William S. Burroughs

PORT OF SAINTS

William S. Burroughs

PORT OF SAINTS

Blue Wind Press : Berkeley : 1980

SIXTH PRINTING

97 98 99 00 01 02 9 8 7 6

LIBRARY OF CONGRESS CATALOGING IN PUBLICATION DATA:

Burroughs, William S   1914 – 1997
Port of saints.

"This new edition...has been extensively rewritten and revised by the author."
I. Title.
PZ4.B972Po [PS3552.U75] 813'.54 80-10309

ISBN 0-912652-64-0 Cloth
ISBN 0-912652-65-9 Paper

Blue Wind Press   Box 7175   Berkeley, California 94707 USA

CONTENTS

M'importa tú y tú 'y tú
I am concerned with you and you and you
Y nada mas que Tuuuuuu
And nothing else but Youuuuuuuuuuuuuuuuuu

I been working on the railroad
All the livelong day
I been working on the railroad
Just to pass the time away
I had a dog his name was Bill
Working on the railroad
He went away but I'm here still
Working on the railroad

Meet me in St. Louis Louie
Meet me at the fair
Don't tell me the lights are shining
Any place but there

Day is done
Gone the sun
From the lake
From the hill
From the sky
All is well
Soldier brave
God is nigh

Oh oh what can the matter be
Johnny's so long at the fair

The only tune that he could play
Was over the hills and far away

When Mr. Wilson, the American Consul, arrived at his office he noticed a young man sitting by the reception desk, and he hoped that whatever the young man wanted could be handled by the Vice Consul, Mr. Carter.

The man at the reception desk said "Good morning" and passed him the slip. He frowned slightly, glanced at the young man who looked back steadily, and walked up a flight of stairs to his office without reading the slip. It was Monday, the mail stacked on his desk. He spread the slip out. The phone rang. An inquiry from the English Consulate—"Yes uh—I don't quite understand what—hmm yes—no not on a tourist visa—" He glanced down at the slip—Name J. Kelly—"No only on a residence visa" Purpose of visit—'Identity'—What on Earth could that mean? Oh

God not a lost passport—"You're quite welcome." He hung up, and flicked a switch. "I will see Mr. Kelly now."

Wednesday, Harbor Beach 2, March 4, 1970

It was a morning in late May, the 26, I think—a cold clear day, wind from the lake. I had walked down to the railroad bridge to fish in the deep pool underneath it. Too cold to sit still, I gave up the idea of fishing and wound my line back onto a spool which I wrapped in oil cloth and shoved into my hip pocket. I could feel someone behind me and I turned around. It was a boy of about my own age. I recognized him as one of the summer people, but they don't usually come until late June. He had a dreamy absent look about him as if he'd stepped out of a painting . . . Saturday Railroad Bridge.

The scrotal egg hatched a black baby out—his name is John . . . a great lake wraiths of wind we came to a valley dark ravine pale blue summer far away . . . Know who I am? (Illegible) picking flowers dust on the window plants and fruit all around ink shirt flapping . . . there was an evil sad as stagnant flowers . . . dead fish a boy swimming the stork's nest a cottage window the things to come white pissoir harbor bells . . .

It was bitterly cold on the wharf, clear and bright in the late sunshine. The fresh offshore breeze had dropped somewhat when John reached the Mary Celeste. He had signed on as third mate.

"Yes Mr.—" The Consul glanced down at the slip though of

course he had memorized the name—"Mr. uh Kelly—and what
can I do for you?"

The young man sitting across the desk had a suntanned face
and very pale grey eyes. 'A merchant seaman' the Consul decided,
removing from his face any trace of warmth—'Lost his money and
passport in a whorehouse.'

"I understood it was you who wanted to see me."

"I—" The Consul was disconcerted. He remembered something about a passport left as security for a bill—Kelly was it? He
looked for the slip in a letter basket, ah here it was—passport No.
32 USA left as security—Hotel Madrid—the Consul was very severe now.

"May I see your passport please?"

To his surprise the young man immediately handed over a
passport which he had apparently held concealed behind the desk.
The Consul examined the passport. It was a seaman's passport,
No. 18—"Hmm these low numbers—date of birth 1944. San Francisco—" The Consul looked up.

"Hello . . . I've been watching you fish. I knew you wouldn't
catch anything. It's too cold."

"You can catch fish through the ice in winter."

"Oh that's different . . . not on cold spring days like this with
a wind."

"You're right I guess. It was just I had nothing else to do."

"You don't have to do anything. When you learn that, you'll
have plenty to do. More than you can keep up with sometimes. . . ."

We have stripped down and there is a taste of metal in my
mouth and this prickling starts in my toes. The boy is standing
there—he brings his finger up in three jerks and his cock comes

up with it, pubic hairs glistening in the dirty yellow light, shadows muttering sex words. . . .

"Of course upstairs if you can make it up there the air is thin you understand pale horse pale rider. . . ."

"The Blue Indians of North Carolina greet you from a West that is dying. . . ."

The three young men, massive blue flesh matured to a hint of decay . . . powder smoke back across the face powder smoke and brown hair the Burroughs childhood fumbling in dying brother sputtered out with exploded star shooting from the hip iridescent head framed in wet leaves purple twilight under the wheeling vultures his cough against my back the thin body feeling the bones . . . He was in love with the cobbled roads and the peaceful ghost child there and the whole park to wander in—Oh Audrey would be content there with an occasional Mexican double, his books in the afternoon to say 'goodbye'. Showed me his code diary for that belated morning. He was looking at something a long time ago.

He looked at John, his lips flecked with blood—smiling as he licked the blood in with the last red rays of the setting sun his face blazed like a comet and dimmed out as the sun sank behind a cloud over Halifax—(Cut in the Halifax Explosion 1910)

"There has been a mistake here. It was a different Kelly I wanted to see."

The young man nodded. "I know that. My brother."

"You knew about it did you? Then why did you come instead of your brother?"

"My brother Joe Kelly is dead."

"Dead? But when? Why hasn't the Consulate been informed?"

"He died five years ago."

The Consul prided himself on his imperturbability. He studied the slip, recalling that it had come to his desk just as he was leaving the office on Friday afternoon—"Well Mr. Kelly, obviously there is some mistake all round. After all it is not an uncommon name. What makes you think this notice refers to your brother in any case?"

"Is the notice dated?"

"Come along to the cottage and have some tea and cake." We were walking back up the tracks, the wind in our faces.

"Let the wind blow through you."

I felt a lightness in my legs as if my body were blowing away. At the same time a pull in my crotch—I was getting hard. He stopped me with a hand on my arm and turned me around to face him, looking down where my pants stuck out at the fly.

"Oh Kiki . . ." Smell of young nights smell of dry parks opens his asshole sunrise St. Louis morning one foot in sweat sock flesh memories away into the distance came in the toilet . . . boulders flowers stretched away to sky on a fish walked in blue years ago let me tell you about ferns and trees the grey dead light two faces water and frogs vague blurred thing in the water that hand frayed scar tissue star dust in the air I ran away from the broken film after that the cold started like dead leaves through the dream drifting the way things fit together pants leans back eating peanuts stands over me naked electric silence and the smell of cock now I am coming in silver flares this long ago address . . .

The shadow of night falls on the boy's face, on the rigging and the circling gulls. John felt the chill of empty space. The boy's face was covered with a white crust of frost and splinters of ice glittered in his ruffled hair, voice eerie and ghostly in the twilight . . .

"Dated? Why, it came to the office Friday afternoon."
"Yes but does it have a date on it?"
The Consul looked at the slip. The date was smudged, illegible. In fact, the Consul had to concede there was something odd
about the notice. It seemed to be a photostatic copy, like some old
document from a forgotten attic, stating simply that the Hotel
Madrid was holding Passport 32 issued in the name of one Joe
Kelly, born Feb. 6, 1944, San Francisco, California—for/against
nonpayment of Hotel Bill (amount not specified), signed by the
manager J. P. Borjurluy. The Consul pursed his lips and picked up
the phone.

I was walking on the rail behind him, leaning into the wind.
"Over there." He pointed across a field.
We slid down a steep gravel slope and walked through the
field to a wooden fence with a gate. It was the usual summer cottage, with split-log walls and a shingle roof. The back door opened
into the kitchen, which contained a wooden table and kerosene
stove. He lit the stove and made coffee in a blue coffee pot and
served it in two white mugs. He put a jar of cookies on the table.
The only sound in the kitchen was the crunch of cookies in our
mouths.
"I will show you my workshop."

Things to come . . . the way things fit together asshole sunrise St. Louis morning outside stands over me naked one foot in a
sweat sock rubbing my cock . . . windy streets the dashboard hand
gun black out his name is John sad stagnant St. Louis morning
outside . . . aliens the human shell is thin she made my bed au

revoir my cock's hard blurred wraiths of wind the boy came in the toilet boulders in the dark ravine pale blue summer sky on a fish . . . What did I pay them? Know who I am?

A chill settled over John's recognition. "Audrey the ice boy."
Frost on his face splinters of ice glittered in his hair virginal lust naked in the last red light a piece of bread at the boy's feet. The boy dimmed out in the rigging and circling gulls.

"I have a notice here—" He read the notice over the phone. "When did that come in? Friday—at what time?—and who brought it? Hmm." He hung up.
"Well this is odd. Seems the man at the desk had stepped out for a moment and found the notice on his desk when he returned . . . Mr. Kelly, could you tell me the circumstances of your brother's death?"
"S.S. Panama out of Casablanca for Copenhagen—went down with all hands."

We went down steep wooden stairs into the basement which was quite light since the cottage was built on a slope and there were large windows across one end of the basement. Under the window was a wooden bench littered with ship models. There was also a sort of pistol with rubber bands, and a dummy about two feet high, made of copper wire in intricate coils. He touched the dummy, running his hands over it, and turned to me.
"Hold out your hand."

Illegible years ago. Let me tell you about a score of years' dust on the window ink shirt flapping down the lost streets vague blurred child sad as stagnant flowers dead hand frayed scar tissue there by the stork's nest a cottage window—

"Little inks to blow into the corpse doesn't it?"

Silver cobwebs from the broken film forgotten places falling slowly like dead leaves through the winter pissoir harbor bells sand in the wind drifting across the street smell of dry parks opens his pants and leans back eating peanuts there in the dark room blue electric silence and the smell of ozone rubbed the mirror ointment on a silver rectum shimmered and flickered together silver spasm exploded in the star dust of the sky—

"I'm Audrey your chill of interstellar space John."

Seemed not to notice the cold as Audrey pointed with his left hand. His eyes lit up inside like a topping forest fire. Smiled like an animal virginal from remote seas of past time plaintive sad survival a musky smell drifted from his open years waiting for this.

"I'm John."

Wind across the boy's face pale on the wharf. He coughed into his handkerchief.

It so happened that the Consul was a collector of sea disasters, on which he kept a scrapbook of clippings. The Mary Celeste, The Great Easter, The Morro Castle. Here was one he had missed—minor perhaps, small freighter, however in view of—he glanced at the slip—decidedly worth looking into. He took out a package of Players, smiling for the first time, and offered the open package to his visitor. The young man accepted a cigarette with a deadpan 'thanks'. There was, the Consul decided, something, well, *remarkable* about the pale cold eyes that seemed to be looking at some distant point far away and long ago. 'He is looking through a telescope' the Consul decided, with a certainty that surprised him.

"I gather your brother was a member of the crew?"

"Yes. He was the third mate."

Brass echo tropical jeers from Panama City wheeling vultures . . .

Numero Uno

Blue blaze of Mexican sky, wheeling vultures . . .

"M'importe NU y NU y NU

Y nada mas que NUUUUUUUU"

Backdrop of mountains—a crowded bus driving at top speed crosses and flowers here and there by the roadside commemorate previous accidents. The bus is packed with Indians inside and on the roof all singing.

"M'importe NU y NU y NU

Y nada mas que NUUUUUUUU"

Chickens squawking, goats bleating, a captive iguana with its mouth sewed shut pisses in silent terror. Two pimps are smoking a joint with a cop. The driver is singing and keeping time with his feet, smoking a thick joint and drinking from a bottle of tequila with one hand. Beside him a leaky tin of gasoline shimmers in the sun. Suddenly a sheet of flame flashes down from his cigarette to the can of gasoline. He glances down and sees what has happened and what he has to do.

Still singing "Y nada mas que NUUUUUUUU" he opens the door and plunges out rolling in a soft ditch by the side of the road and lands on his feet, light as a cat. The bus plunges into a narrow ravine and bursts into flame. Screams and burning flesh on the wind. Only those on top of the bus can save themselves. Workers cutting cane with machetes drop their bundles of cane. They look at the burning bus and they look at the driver. Survivors from the roof are also looking at the driver. With inhuman speed, dodging, stiff-arming, he takes off across the mountains, outdistancing his sixty pursuers.

Old Sarge, addressing a graduating class of cadets: "You boys think you are superior to the local earth gooks, don't you? Well now you'll have a chance to prove it . . ." (He hands out scripts. The cadets look at them in horror.)

Cadet 1: "You mean I have to set the bus on fire and jump out right in front of sixty machetes?"

Old Sarge: "That's right. Should be easy for Shifty Sawyer the End Run Kid."

Cadet 2: "Rush into the first lifeboat in drag and fight off fifty women?"

Old Sarge: "Teach you all about the sex enemy Buster."

Cadet 3: "Sneak a parachute on board a passenger plane, bail out and let the plane crash? Why, I could lose my wings for a thing like that."

Old Sarge: "Stop moaning flyboy or you'll be back in the infantry."

Cadet 4: "Guess I drew the easy one—find suitable accomplices and hold up any branch of the Banco Nacionale."

Old Sarge: "That's what *you* get for not being good at anything . . . All right you jokers you can get your kits now . . . cyanide rings, tie pins, pen injectors, teeth . . . old shit but good . . . and other poisons that require less volume . . . this cigarette lighter shoots botulism pellets . . . takes effect twelve hours later. Now for the biologicals . . . all the old standbys . . . anthrax, bubonic plague, typhus lice . . . and these new R for Radioactive strains . . . be careful with these . . . no vaccine . . . have to stay out of your fallout. And these capsules . . . take one and for the next six hours your breath will knock out a back room of tough cops . . . one of these and your farts will take out a precinct. And this drug NU will give you superhuman performance for six hours . . . you can bend iron bars, stick your fist through a door, run fifty miles an hour . . . but when it wears off you are helpless as a baby for six days . . . so use that energy to find a place to land . . .

"And here's your script Audrey . . . You're the writer. Well, write a wild boy takeover. You can start in a modest way with the state of New Mexico, using your old radioactive Alma Mater Los Alamos as your headquarters . . ."

As the vigilantes of Norms led by Mike Finn streamed into the Parry Reservation, a great cry of rage went up: the Parries were gone. Spitting hate at the empty space, they killed all the animals they could find and then began looking at each other . . .

"What are you looking at so funny Jed? You can read my mind maybe?"

"You seem to know more about that sort of thing than I do Homer."

Several hundred thousand Norms slaughtered each other on the spot. Then Mike Finn took over: "We must pull up the very concept of Paranormal experience by its infected roots."

He organized a vast Thought Police. Anybody with an absent-minded expression was immediately arrested and executed. Anyone who expressed any ideas that deviated in any way from decent church-going morality suffered the same fate. The American Moral Disease passed into its terminal stage. Laughing was strictly forbidden. Everyone wore identical expressions of frustrated hate looking for a target. Then came the news that everyone longed to hear: "The Parries are back. They are established in a city of towers and turrets on the site of Los Alamos."

To a vast chorus of Onward Christian Soldiers the Norms marched on Los Alamos. They did not use atom bombs because there was nobody left who could use one. The atomic physicists and technicians had been purged as Parries because folks couldn't understand their formulae. Planes had been grounded because pilots flying around might become Parries. Under the rule of Mike Finn it didn't pay to be good at anything. In consequence the whole structure of Western society had collapsed.

Armed with scythes and pitchforks and shotguns they marched, killing every living thing in their path. They were swarming up the mesa now, screaming with rage.

TOWERS OPEN FIRE

The Yellow Serpent and the Spitting Cobra opened up with all the hate ever spit from decent church-going eyes, religious cops, the whole cesspool of the Bible Belt belted back like white lightning—

DEATH DEATH DEATH

That host withered and dropped like flies in flytox. The Blue Mongoose danced in for the kill and the way back was blocked by the Exterminator. Dazed survivors stumbled about in a pile of corpses from Los Alamos to Illinois as wave after wave of invaders swept down from the Bering Straits and up from the Mexican border destroying every vestige of the American nightmare, leveling the hideous cities and slaughtering the surviving Norms like cattle with the aftosa. Anyone who used the words RIGHT and WRONG was IMMEDIATELY KILLED. The Norms were then ploughed under for fertilizer.

Camera pans the scattered forces and broken morale of the militants . . . teenage alcoholics, underground press closing down, black panthers finished, censorship coming back, pollution, overpopulation, atomic tests . . .

VENCEREMOS?

"We're going to hang out our washing
On the Siegfried line
If the Siegfried line's still there . . ."

Audrey's arrival in Mexico . . . April 3, 1973. Room 18, 8 Duke St., St. James extends and opens at the sides. Outside, trees and a river bed with a thin trickle of water—pools here and there—a highway in the distance. There are two boys in the room. Now the door opens and a third boy comes in. He is about fifteen, wearing a blue coat and grey flannel pants.

"Are you dead?" Audrey asks.

"Yes," the boy says. He is critical of the other boys and of Audrey.

Audrey asks, "Do you all think you could have done a better job?"

The boy says yes. Boy number 1, who has been there the longest, tries to pull number 3 onto the bed. Number 3 braces himself and says, "Keep away." Meanwhile the Banco Nacionale has been robbed on the highway. Audrey decides to go to the police. They set out driving through empty streets. Number 1 asks him what the Chief of Police actually does . . .

"All sorts of things. He throws people in jail and beats them up. He is also responsible for the whole police force, who are always getting drunk and shooting each other and the citizens. He must maintain discipline."

We arrive in a courtyard and boy number 2, who speaks Spanish, goes in to arrange an interview. We are ushered into a very small office. Filing cabinets, a bench along one side. A lady magistrate sits at a small desk with a typewriter in front of her, a window behind her. The bench runs under the desk, so that when Audrey sits down his legs are under the desk, almost touching her knees. Number 1 perches on a filing cabinet opposite Audrey on the other side of the desk. Number 2 sits to Audrey's left with his arms folded. Number 3 stands leaning against a filing cabinet. The lady magistrate is a solidly built woman of about sixty with a large pale face, a prominent nose, steelrimmed glasses and thin lips. She has more the look of a scholar than a magistrate.

Audrey is prepared for questions about the robbery . . . did he hear shots? etc. . . . also for questions about his relationship with the three boys. However, she begins obliquely to speak of the matter of trust . . . she expects trust from him. Francis Huxley, for example, has done a translation of _____, a Spanish name . . . Audrey is about to say "Oh yes very well done . . ." He realizes that she is telepathic. He realizes also that for some reason Francis Huxley is in solid with her and he is not. She goes on in the same oblique, vaguely critical vein. He realizes suddenly that any reference to the robbery is somehow out of place. She then asks the three boys to speak. Number 1 grins and speaks of 'societal somnolence.' She is displeased by this and purses her thin lips in disapproval. Number 2 says "We have come to help"—catches himself just in time from the social blunder of referring to the robbery. Number 3 says nothing, but clearly he is the one most in her favor.

We are now free to go, but she indicates that we are under surveillance—of a sort, that is . . .

Defeated and pursued, with only a handful of followers left, Audrey invokes a curse on the White Goddess and all her works, from the Conquistadores to Hiroshima, from the Bog People to the Queen, from Dixie to South Africa . . . a curse from all the little people of the earth: DEATH TO THE WHITE GODDESS. The boys decide to take refuge in Mexico, where one of them has an uncle.

Rundown hacienda in Mexico, mountain stronghold of the

once-powerful De Carson family. The family has lost ground lately, perhaps because of an old-fashioned sense of honor which has presumably put them at a disadvantage in competition with American methods used by their opponents. Now they are preparing a comeback. Tio Mate, the family pistolero, has been summoned by the young Don.

"Take care of the so inconvenient Vestiori family, and smile only when absolutely convenient . . ."

Tio Mate smiles . . .

The moment is now propitious to bring up the matter of his young nephew and his friends. The young Don is interested. He asks for particulars.

Flashback shows the wild boys mowed down by cold eyed narcs and Southern lawmen backed by religious women and big money.

The young Don quotes . . . "Battles are fought to be won and this is what happens when you lost . . ."

Tio Mate: "Survivors have learned this kindergarten lesson . . . They could be valuable . . ."

Looking into the skull he sees the boys as this lance . . . a spear of stars across the sky . . . a lance can also be a LACK . . . hummmmmyes the precise uh dead child . . . immune to death . . . immune to birth . . . if we could cut off the supply of uh male issue?

Lawmen disappear from a Southern street . . . insolent youths black and white bar the way of a Southern Belle . . . they take her bag of groceries and strip her clothes off, camping around in her drag . . .

The young Don caresses the skull ... a sweet sour musky flower smell drifts from the skull ... a nitrous ozone smell laced with stomach-grabbing whiffs of carrion and cyanide ...

Buzzards eating a dead cow in a hot Mexican landscape ... Condemned man in gas chamber. His face changes into the face of the White Goddess ...

A musty dry smell of deserted outhouses and empty locker rooms ... a humid rotten flower smell ... the smell of mutation ...

As the skull smell fills the room cats and foxes and weasels and coyotes and raccoons and minks slink into the room and rub themselves against the furniture and the legs of the young Don and Tio Mate ...

The smell of the skull is the trademark of the De Carson family. There have been many attempts to steal the skull ... Tio Mate has 18 deer on his gun.

The young Don nods and looks into the crystal skull. Camera tracks into the skull, tracing the convolutions of his plan. His family is losing to the American invasion. Soon there will be no families like his. But if he could throw a lance straight into the heart of the *American White Whale*? Into the heart of the *White Goddess*?

Here is the young District Attorney just up from the capitol. Tio Mate drops by to give him a lesson in folklore.

Tio Mate: "You know señor abogado I am going to send you a deer."

D.A.: "Oh really that's very kind of you but please do not give yourself so much trouble . . ."

Tio Mate: "It is my pleasure señor abogado."

Horse with dead man draped over saddle like a dead deer is led to the police post by a stolid Mexican cop.

He jerks his thumb back matter-of-factly as the D.A. comes to the door:

"Un venado."

Now the D.A. understands this expression peculiar to rural Mexico. Across the blue Mexican sky and black buzzard wings, Tio Mate smiles . . .

> Tio Mate is come to call
> Un venado? No trouble at all
> Across blue sky and empty miles
> Tio Mate smiles

Inspired by the skull, the boys roll around in Mexico like cats in catnip. Willy the Actor gets himself up like a macho in the days of Président Alemán—glen plaid suit, false mustache, pearl-handled .45. He careens through the streets in a black Cadillac screaming "CHINGOA" as he blasts at cats and chickens with his .45. Now the Cadillac screams to a stop in front of a neon-lit cocktail bar. He gets out with Audrey and Jerry in drag as Chapultepec movie starlets, one on each arm, and staggers into the bar singing

> "ANDO BORRACHO
> ANDO TOMANDO

YAHHHHOOOOOOOOOOOOOWWWWWWWWWW"

The bartender turns greener. This looks like trouble. The bar is lit in green neon with a tank of tropical fish along one wall. A party of American tourists stands at the bar. Willy stares at a blonde girl in slacks.

"Buenas noches *señorita!*"

She turns her back on him. He edges closer and gooses her with his .45. Jerry and Audrey titter and nudge each other.

"Isn't he *marvelous* . . . Never repeats himself."

A crew-cut American youth starts to intervene. Willy shifts the .45, levels it at his stomach, and smiles. Another American is edging towards the phone booth.

"CHINGOA!"

Willy blasts the glass front of the phone booth and shatters the phone into fragments.

"Never repeats himself."

Now another boy got up as a macho gets out of a Cadillac and staggers in with two blondes and a troop of mariachi singers. The two machos rush into each other's arms, pounding each other on the back.

"RODRIGUEZ"

"BÉRNABE"

"CABRÓN"

They give the Grito, which is taken up by the mariachi singers, who go into 'Ando Borracho.'

Bérnabe throws money on the bar and orders Old Pharr Scotch for the house. He turns to the American tourists.

"Practically everybody in Mexico drinks Scotch."

"Never repeats himself." (This litany is taken up by the four blondes.)

Now they go into a Mexican cop shake-down act. Bérnabe pops a huge embossed golden badge into his mouth and snarls his lips back from it.

"Never repeats himself."

They make the round of the bar, Bérnabe flashing the badge while Rodriguez holds passports upside down, glaring at them suspiciously and belching garlic.

"Papers very bad Meester . . . You come along to the Comisária."

"Never repeats himself."

Bérnabe leaps up onto a table and pisses into the fish tank.

"Never repeats himself."

They put on Charro costumes and ride around terrorizing the local peons. They stage dossin' contests, sitting along a wall with hats over their eyes to see who can sit the longest and move the least. Davy Jones wins these contests hands down.

Now they get out the Aztec and Mayan Codices and camp around in Moctezuma feather robes. Codex shows someone spitting out flint . . . hard words . . . Mayan codex shows a little green scroll coming out of mouth. Audrey and Davy Jones sit opposite each other, Audrey in a hummingbird robe, Davy Jones as a Black Captain. Davy Jones spits out flint arrow-heads. Audrey blows out a little green paper scroll which bursts in a reek of rotten eggs. This gives him an idea and he sets to work with molds and hard candy. The candy is ready. Naked except for his hummingbird robe, flanked by Jerry in a bulging loincloth, he sweeps into a bar where a macho is drinking. The macho looks at them and spits on the floor.

"MARICONES."

Audrey spits a candy on the bar which slides along and stops in front of the macho. A little figure labeled YO is fucking a woman labeled TU MADRE. There it is on the bar . . . "CHINGO TU MADRE" (I FUCK YOUR MOTHER). As the macho stares in disbelief another candy slides down in front of him . . . a church with the label EN.

"I FUCK YOUR MOTHER IN CHURCH."

"CHINGOA!"

The macho reaches for his .45 and stops, as Audrey swings a sawed-off shotgun out from under his robe and levels it steadily at the macho stomach.

The scandal of Los Niños Locos is bringing the De Carson family into disrepute with their neighbors. The boys plan a farewell performance.

Independence Day . . . All the vecinos, pistoleros, rancheros, peons, opium growers and policías gather in the town square in front of the Governor's Palace waiting to give the Grito. On the roof of the Palace the boys appear, naked except for gunbelts and .45's, fucking each other in plain sight of the crowd. As they come, they give the Grito and blast vultures out of the sky which rain down into the square, spattering the citizens with carrion. As the enraged crowd storms the palace the boys make their escape in a huge glider in the shape of a vulture powered by six motorcycle engines. The time has come for the boys to travel.

The film *Quiemada*, which is Portuguese for 'burnt' . . . set in early 19th century on a West Indian island. Marlon Brando as Sir William, an agent of the British government, gets off a boat.

"Your bags sir?"

The porter is José Dolores. He tries to steal Sir William's suitcase. Sir William finds him, and after a disciplinary session decides that this is the boy he wants to get the Portuguese out. Sir William organizes a gold robbery and a rebellion with José Dolores as the rebel leader. Time passes, and José is now leading a guerrilla band against the sugar plantations. This is hitting them in the tea in England, so they call in Sir William to put down the rebellion, which he does with thousands of British troops looking rather like a turnout from the White Bear my dear only *relatively* well-trained and well-armed against a handful of guerrillas—it's a massacre. Not one British soldier is lost.

José is captured alive. Sir William tries to save him and persuade him to escape, but he prefers a martyr's role and is hanged by inept black hangmen. Sir William has to show them how to tie the noose. Then he rides away. Now we are back at the beginning but he is leaving, not arriving, with the same bags after ten years.

"Your bags sir?"

He turns and sees a black boy so much like José he does a double take and starts to smile, "Juan, it's you . . ."

The boy sticks a knife in his side just as José is being hanged. He falls and workers go on unloading in sepia for a few seconds seen through dying eyes and stop as a woman dumps a bag of flour on the quay. FREEZE.

Where will Father William go?

How many times he must have thought 'why that dumb bush nigger—I could show him how to bring the whole Antilles to its knees—with the weapons of sabotage, poison, and assassination no white man is safe from his servants. Europe needs sugar and rum—how about that? Got the Royal Navy where they live. He could learn to *use* white technicians; get their skills and learn to do it better, welding the technical knowledge of the whites with the immediate present-time aptitude of the blacks. The Antilles? Why stop there? A sugar monopoly of the whole West Indian area.' Sadly Sir William shakes his head. 'He'd never trust me or learn from me, and if he did, I'd be out of the picture. Spengler foresaw that blacks led by white adventurers would take over Western Europe and the United States. Spengler was a white idiot if he thought the blacks would ever accept such leadership, even if they could win by doing so. Now,' Sir William decides, 'I would have to be black.'

This can be arranged.

Cut back to Sir William as a young agent. The chief has asked him into his office for a little chat. The chief seems embarrassed. He mixes a whisky and puts on a father-about-to-tell-his-son-about-sex act.

"How old are you William?'

"Twenty-three sir."

"Oh yes—humm—well, old enough to hear about the facts of death. Now I know you've already heard a lot from the boys at Downside, and the padres and I can tell you they don't know one fucking thing about flying."

"Flying sir?"

"Yeah son, from one landing field to another. You're old enough to know the facts of death, son, and what they told you at school—the whisky priests—is like trying to fly a jet plane with all the wrong directions. You won't get that Jesus Christ off the runway. And the when-you're-dead-you're-dead lads are even worse. The deader you think you will be, the worse place you land in. Well now you learn to pick your spot and your landing field and set it up, you understand?"

Fragile gliders take off across an abyss. This freezes into a painting—THE ARRIVAL written in golden letters on the frame.

The time has come for the boy to travel—in time . . .

We will rewrite all the wrongs of history. We will kill all the shits before they can be born.

Their first trip takes them back to a West Indian island in 1845. They use the film *Quiemada* as a springboard and land as military advisers to a handful of guerrillas equipped with flintlock rifles and led by José Dolores. The guerrillas have reached a standoff with the slovenly Portuguese. This gives the advisers time. However, British troops equipped with the new percussion lock rifles are on the way. They will be led by Sir William Walker, an expert in guerrilla warfare. How to build effective weapons from the materials available? There is iron ore in the area occupied by the guerrillas. There is still time.

Old Sarge: "All right you jokers we're going to build *weapons* . . . I mean weapons designed to kill." He holds up a flintlock rifle. "Not designed to blow up in your face and not work when it rains and only kill one enemy at a time at 50 feet if the wind is right . . . We have iron ore and we have time. Sure, Sir William is on his way with his redcoats. By the time Sir William gets out here and gets the brilliant idea that we need a source of supplies, namely the local villagers, and moves out the villagers and burns down the villages, we will be ready for his redcoats. First step in inventing anything new is to forget what you already know—forget everything you know about springs, triggers, machine-made parts, and concentrate on firepower. How to get the most killing power from where you are to where they are. Now a few general principles: the bigger they are, the easier they are to make. It is much easier to make a good cannon than a good handgun. So let's make some big ones first. Making big ones will show us how to make them smaller and more portable. Look at what the enemy does not have, the thing they don't have is the easiest for you to build. Well I'll tell you boys, it's a *firecracker*. Six hundred years of firearms and they never learned to use a *firecracker*. By that I mean an exploding projectile, whether thrown by hand, propelled from a launcher, or fired from a cannon. Now, they had grenades and even mortars in the 17th century but they couldn't see the extensions. Six hundred years of cannon balls and did it ever occur to them to have a cannon ball that explodes on contact? Like I say, they never learned to use the *firecracker*. Would you believe me boys, the first crude grenade designed to explode on contact appeared in the American Civil War?

"And this grenade was a hideous thing. The explosive core was covered with nipples and on the end of each nipple a percussion cap. This core was loosely encased in an iron shell. On contact the percussion caps would hit the iron shell and explode the grenade. Many went off before that. Any jerky movement in throwing the grenade and it went off in your face. You had to use a gentle bowling motion. Well, we can do a lot better than that without percussion caps, and that is our first weapon and the easiest to make: grenades. Grenades and grenade launchers. These can be of any size from a handgun to a cannon.

"Fortunately for us, the stupidity of the military mind is unbelievable—otherwise they would already have weapons we could not duplicate without setting up factories. Now we have a grenade, which is simply a metal casing with powder inside it. We want that grenade to go off when it gets where we throw or propel it. There are many ways to do this, but few so ill-advised as the artifact I have just described. Remember, we do not have fulminate of mercury." As Old Sarge talks, the young faces shift and change. And as he talks the devices he describes are being constructed . . .

"Now the simplest way to explode a grenade is with an external fuse. Fuses blow out and we do not have material to make good fuses. We can of course use a fuse encased in a metal tube flush with the surface of the grenade, the exposed powder sealed with wax so the powder does not drop out. Another simple solution is wires passing through the shell of the grenade into the powder charge and protruding from the surface. Pitch, or rags soaked in oil wrapped around the grenade and lighted, will heat up the wires and explode the charge. Allowance must be made for different ranges. A way must be found to time the explosion. One way is to cover the wires with varying degrees of insulation—sealing wax for example: so many dips in sealing wax. So the thickness of the wax on the wires gives us a fair approximation as to how long it will take for those wires to heat up and explode the charge. Generally speaking you want to get your ignition mechanism *inside* the grenade; the less parts you have sticking out of the grenade the better. One solution is to have the metal wall of the grenade very thin in places. Those spots then heat up quicker and explode the charge, and the thickness determines how long this will take.

"Now we will construct a grenade designed to explode on contact. The simplest is a head of thin metal that will be shoved back on contact. This head is loaded with flint chips and iron filing, so that when it is shoved back a spark will ignite the charge. Phosphorus match heads can also be used if you remember to keep your shell out of the sun, preferably in a simple evaporation style refrigerator. The flint can be attached to a plunger that is forced down on contact. Now your grenade will explode on contact with any solid object including flesh.

"Now let's turn our attention to this piece of pipe they call a gun—and they called it that for three hundred years before the idea of getting it all into one cartridge occurred to them. So let's make a cartridge without fulminate of mercury. Here is a cartridge with a wire where the cap would ordinarily be. The wire extends into the powder charge. This wire needs only to be heated up to explode the charge. Curiously enough one of the simplest ways to do this is with an electric battery, so one of our first attempts is a battery gun. And we are not going to start with a single shot, we are going to start with a repeater. And we will make a big one first, which will show us how to make smaller ones. We can call this a heat gun, since all we need is heat to heat up the wire and ignite the charge. This one requires two men to operate and must be fired from a tripod or an installation. The magazine is a steel frame in which the cartridges are fitted. This is then pulled by hand through the breech of the gun and held in place there until the cartridge explodes. The charge is exploded by a battery, or it can be exploded by a box behind the breech filled with hot coals, by a kerosene lamp or even by a magnifying glass in sunlight. All you need is heat. Just bring the wire in contact with the hot plate, sight, and wait for the shot. You don't need a trigger and you don't need a hammer. You will see now why we skipped the single shot. It is literally easier to fire such a gun with a magazine where you pull the magazine through the breech (later of course we will have revolving magazines or magazines that move on springs) than it is to insert and fire a single cartridge.

"We deliberately choose for this mission personnel with inventive minds but with no experience as gunsmiths and no clear idea as to the parts involved in a modern rifle or revolver. In the progress of any invention problems arise, and the way in which these problems are solved determines the whole future form of the invention as soon as it goes into mass production. Now the solution of the technical problem may not have been the best solution or even a good solution. You see we are already in process of eliminating two parts of a gun that were thought to be essential—namely, the trigger and the hammer. So the rifles and handguns that will emerge from these models when it is possible to produce machine parts will be considerably different from modern small arms. The same considerations apply to any invention. For example, the simplest form of motor is a jet—why bog down in cylinders, carburetors, and spark plugs?

"Another substitute for a percussion cap is a phosphorus match head sealed into the cartridge. This can be ignited by scraping against the breech. The motion of bringing the cartridge into the breech also explodes the cartridge. And why must the cap be at the end of the cartridge? Why not on top toward the front? If cap is in front, the back of the cartridge can be thicker to absorb recoil and the whole breech construction can be simplified."

Sir William arrives now, with his redcoats equipped with the then-new percussion-lock single-shot muzzle-loading rifles. They are given a banquet by the Governor. The French Consul emits a sharp cold bray of laughter. "I drink to the glorious victory of the brave English over two hundred ragged half starved guerrillas armed with flintlocks and machetes."

As Sir William advances burning villages, the guerrillas fall
back. Now he has them boxed in at the head of a valley, a sheer
drop to the sea behind them, another English ship standing by. Six
hundred men and officers, the officers on horseback, move into
the valley.

"Into the valley of death rode the six hundred . . ."

They are careless and sure of victory, still out of range of the
old rifles the guerrillas are presumed to have. As the first shower
of grenades arch over their heads, the regimental joker calls out:

"The monkeys are throwing coconuts . . ."

Everybody laughs and ducks.

"Horse and hero fell . . ."

Sir William's horse rears and saves Sir William's life as a grenade explodes directly in front of it. Sir William gets up covered
with horse blood from head to foot.

"SPREAD OUT . . . TAKE COVER . . ."

And now the cannons open up from emplacements. Officers
and men are fleeing in a blind panic. Like a true English gentleman, Sir William bellows the obvious:

"EVERY MAN FOR HIMSELF"

"Cannon to the right of them, cannon to the left of them vol-
leyed and thundered."

"And then they rode back . . ." Those who still had a horse
under them shit sure did. Others ran, walked, hobbled and
crawled back.

"But not the six hundred . . ."

Two hundred and twenty-three hysterical shellshocked survivors made it back to base . . . (Le Comte emitted a sharp cold
bray of laughter.)

Camera pans the field as the World War II music hall number
plays in a slow and minor key . . .

"We're going to hang out our washing
On the Siegfried line
If the Siegfried line's still there . . ."

Audrey and the Dib in Atlanta airport. Audrey is a crewcut
young husband, the Dib his pregnant wife. As they are about to
board the plane for Miami they are spotted by a team of FBI men
with orders to take them alive.

"Stop, you two . . ."

Audrey and the Dib sprint for the plane, the agents in pursuit.
The Dib unzips his "baby" and tosses it over his shoulder. A gas is
escaping from the bundle of padding. *Nerve gas.* The pursuing
agents crumple and fall as Audrey and the Dib gain the cockpit of
the plane . . .

"Take off right from here . . ."

Wake of the plane spreads nerve gas through the airport, and
out into the street. People stacked in shitting pissing twitching
heaps. Cars crashing. Police cars rushing up. Cops jump out and
fall . . .

As the plane circles the field, Audrey lets his mouth drop
open like an idiot boy in a 1920 movie as he points:

"Hey lookit all them dead bodies!"

Snow in the streets . . . Audrey is coughing. Police barrier
ahead, youths lined up against a wall, cop there with sawed-off
shotgun. Audrey doubles forward coughing and comes up shooting with the silencered P-.38. Sput Sput Sput . . . a noise like popping champagne corks but not as loud. Police cars everywhere
dodging into doorways . . . They take refuge in a strip club . . .
young boys need it special.

Girl prances out . . . "I've got that je n' sais quoi . . ."

She flips her hand and a claw springs out.

"I'VE GOT THAT I DON'T KNOW WHAT . . ."

Insect fangs break through her face.

"I'VE GOT THAT HUMMMBUBBLERGUBBLLLLLUGH . . ."

The audience rushes for the exits as the horrible black stench of insect mutation fills the room. Police sirens . . . Audrey and the Dib running down alley as police cars block them off. Blank wall ahead . . . Audrey throws the last egg and the wall turns into a transparent membrane. They squeeze through as the cops rush up shooting . . .

Sand in the streets . . . smell of the sea . . . pawn shops . . . We duck into Joe's Lunch and I look around. 1930-40 . . . Thieves, hustlers, junkies. I find that I have a habit. Time travel will bring it on. Spot a junkie and he comes over to the table.

"Don't I know you from some place?"

"Yeah" I said and looked at him. It was coming out his ears.

"You looking to score?"

"Sure."

"I know a croaker will write but he wants a sawski."

"How many?"

"Thirty quarters."

"That wouldn't be Doc Van would it?"

"Well yes. You know him?"

"Not really. Just heard about him."

The junkie looked relieved. "He won't write unless he knows you. I can't take you in to him, you understand."

"I understand . . . Helen still with him?"

"Yeah. She's the bouncer in case anyone tries to muscle him for a script."

"She's well known too."

"Yeah I guess so. Now look, if you can spring for the bread I can hit him right away and meet you back here."

I shook my head and smiled . . . "I'll go with you and wait outside. But right now we want to find a room and park our gear."

He nodded. "This is a hot neighborhood. No good being out in the street." He glanced at my brief case wondering what was in it. I stood up. "Meet you here in half an hour."

The Globe Hotel was on a side street under a scenic railway that wasn't working and looked like it hadn't been used for quite some years. An old Chinese took our money and handed us the key. It was the kind of room you expect in a place like that: double bed, wash stand, wardrobe, green blinds. We stashed the guns and cartridges under the bathtub in the hall bathroom. I felt up under the wash stand and found some junkie's works wrapped in brown paper and shook a roach off it. It had been there a long time. I put it back. I'd be needing it later.

The junkie was waiting in Joe's. He was a little sick now, his eyes watering. He led the way through sand-covered streets. Occasionally a lulow ran across the road.

"You want to be careful" the junkie told me. "One of those fuckers bites you, it gets infected . . . Here we are. Don't let him rumble you waiting."

I stood in a doorway with a pocket telescope and watched where the junkie went and the ring he gave to get in. I'd be paying a professional call on Helen and Van later. Something touched my leg. I looked down and saw a lulow. It snapped at me and caught its teeth in the cuff of my trousers. I pivoted and brought the other foot up and down on the back of its neck. In about fifteen minutes the junkie walked out. I figured he'd been trying to get Van down to a fin. I figured he hadn't got him down, knowing Van. We split the 30 quarters in the doorway over the dead lulow.

Back in the hotel I got the works out of the bathroom. On a hunch the guns as well. You never know how much to take on a time travel habit like this. Best be on the safe side. Too much could slow me down. I decided on three quarters and it was just right. I lay back on the bed with pillows behind my head and did some thinking. Helen and Van . . . abortion and pushing would be just a cover story for those two birds. Van: original nationality Canadian . . . age 57 . . . specialist in transfer operations and transplants . . . he can graft a leper leg on you while you wait . . . debarred from practice in many places under many names . . . always comes back with the fix in . . . must be laying low now with this writing croaker act. Helen: Australian . . . age 60 . . . phenomenal strength in hands and forearms . . . masseuse . . . abortionist . . . torture expert . . . jewel thief . . . multiple murderess. I was going up against two old pros . . . have to watch every move. She'd have a chain on the door of course and it would be a door with iron plates. I needed an angle to get in.

The Dib walked in fast and shut the door. "We got company in the hall . . . narc followed me back from Joe's."

"Just one?"

"Yeah."

Word for word I had my angle from a story in an old pulp magazine I'd read years ago. This gun holed up with the mob after him. Somebody comes in with false whiskers, he uses the whiskers to get out. I had my whiskers . . .

When Audrey stepped into the hall the narc was pretending to look at the name plate on another apartment. Crew cut, dark glasses, blue suit.

"Can I help you Mister?"

As the narc turned around Audrey flipped his gun out and said his piece.

"Up."

Just one word in a quiet voice, but he knew how to say that so anybody would believe it. He held the gun with a slow searching movement up and down the narc's stomach. He licked his lips and shivered. Killer's fever, that's what it was. A raw blood smell steamed off him. Killer's fever, and the narc knew it. He wasn't about to argue.

"Hands behind your head . . . This way." Audrey gestured with the gun. The Dib opened the door. He had a gun in his other hand.

"Sit down over there. Now open your coat . . . now reach down there *slow* with two fingers and ease that gun out and toss it on the bed." The narc did it. Two guns on him now.

"Now your wallet with the badge in it." The narc did it.

"Now stand up."

The Dib slapped him. Then I gave him a shot that would put him out for twelve hours. I put on the dark glasses and stood in front of the tarnished wardrobe mirror. It was so perfect it scared me. And the Dib was perfect as my Italian partner who makes the buys. Ahearn and Barrazini . . . There was a blank search warrant in the wallet. I filled it out. DO NOT DISTURB on the door as we walked out.

There was the door. I gave the special ring I'd spotted when the junkie rang. Three long, two short, one long. No sound from inside. That door was thick. Now the door opened six inches on a chain and Helen looked out . . . Cold grey eyes, hair dyed black. It was like the door of a refrigerator had opened. I threw the gold badge on her. The refrigerator got colder.

"You have a warrant.?" I passed her the warrant.

She looked at it. Then she let the chain down. She wasn't worried. Van wouldn't keep junk on the premises. It wasn't junk I was looking for. As soon as we were inside I shot her twice in the neck and spattered the wall behind her with vertebrae. Down the hall and into Van's surgery. He turned greener when he saw me. He was a narrow shoulders man with wide hips, his skull covered by a greenish fuzz, his face an embalmed pink color which comes from shooting Time Juice. I shot him through the head.

Now to find what we were looking for. Must be in the wall safe. We had the tools. It took about thirty seconds. Sirens outside. Must be bugged. Out the back way, got a cab to the airport. Have to think up a new angle on a skyjack quick. Sure it was easy in those days, but it's burned down now in all directions. We could run into metal detectors, security men, the lot. Here we are and just like I thought, 1970 airport. By now we are prep school kids on vacation.

In the bar I spot Davy Jones and Carl. The bartender won't serve us and we make a little fuss to be sure Carl and Jones raise us and get tickets on the same flight. Flight 895 for Detroit, due to leave in forty-five minutes. Into the head, where we each take a shot of Super P. This drug gives superhuman strength and dexterity for up to six hours. I could feel it pound and tingle through me. I knew I could put my fist right through the shithouse wall into the next booth if I wanted to. And right away I saw how to get guns onto the plane: let the security men carry guns for us and take them away when we were ready.

Out in the waiting room we spot a middle-aged couple on our flight with shopping bags full of coconut heads and stuffed alligators, and slip a gun in. That will show us who the security men are. We go through clean but when that couple hits the booth, bells all over the airport. They are hustled away screaming but the security men think after looking at them the gun might have been planted, and they really bear down on the search. We are half an hour late. By now we know just who they are and where they are sitting.

Half an hour out of Detroit, the Dib and your reporter start down the aisle to the head—a bit of rough air spills us right into their laps. They are out cold and we have the guns before they knew what hit them. That leaves two more with four guns on them and the way that Super P comes out your eyes anybody will believe it when you tell them this plane is skyjacked. We handcuff the security men to their seats and leave Davy Jones to cover the passengers.

Captain Cook looked around and saw the gun in Audrey's hand the frightened face of the stewardess.

"Oh God not again, there must be an easier way to make a living."

"This time is a little bit different. Tell Detroit you are in trouble. Nothing about a skyjack, ketch sabe? This gun wouldn't like it."

"Double Echo to Model T . . . come in please."

"Model T Control to Double Echo . . . Go ahead."

"It looks like we're in trouble here . . ."

"Cut" Audrey jerked a thumb toward Carl. "Meet your new navigator . . ."

Carl pointed to a map. "Right here is where we are going."

"Like I told you this one is a little bit different . . ."

"Can't make it without refueling . . ."

"Just get as close as you can."

The captain shrugged. "We aim to please."

"Good. And we aim to be pleased."

An hour out of Detroit we picked up the tail end of a hurricane as a tail wind. "God is our co-pilot . . . we'll make it now."

"Ever hear about ice on the wings?"

"See if you can make radio contact, Carl."

"Teleport to Frisco . . . come in please . . ." Crackling sounds, faint intermittent voice . . . "Frisco to teleport . . . go ahead . . ."

"On target . . . hour short . . . ice on wings . . ."

"Read you . . . have wings . . . four hundred range . . ."

"We could just make it . . ."

"We're going down right now . . ."

"Radio position. Stay on course . . ."

Nothing ahead but snow . . . "Visibility zero."

They sat there watching the altimeter drop . . . 300 . . . 200 . . . plane dipped . . . 50 . . . touch down . . . a long sickening skid . . . crash . . . stop. The plane was on its side, one wing sheared off . . .

"Radio position . . . should be enough fuel left for a flare."

Fifteen minutes later the two-engine prop plane landed. Back to the base . . . teleport equipment.

Teleport and exteriorization equipment can be constructed by any boy mechanic in his basement workshop. References are

Collected Works of Wilhelm Reich, Journeys Out of the Body by Robert A. Monroe. Basically the equipment consists of *magnetized* iron with organic material outside. The simplest form suitable for such trips in the second body as Monroe describes is an oblong box lined with magnetized iron. You have six surfaces, four sides, top and bottom. These then would be arranged so that some of the magnetic fields are attracting and some opposing. For example, door and back side opposing fields, right and left side attracting, top and bottom opposing. Monroe's description of a circle of vibrations moving up and down the body suggests more elaborate models with moving parts. For example a cylinder consisting of a series of disks alternately opposing and attracting that can rotate in different directions. This model is suitable for actual teleporting as distinct from exteriorization. The subject stands in the middle of the cylinder and controls rotation from a switch. Reclining models are also useful, but for teleporting it is best to start on your feet you jokers.

Audrey started slowly at first, gradually increasing the speed. He experienced the sweet metal taste, erection, then the sensation of flesh whirling off the bones with a sweet toothache pain. Then the pictures . . . he is standing on the mesa of Los Alamos and a wind blows him down the mesa with autumn leaves. Looking back, he sees some boys on a mountain, camped in teepees . . . He goes back against the wind and catches one of the boys as he falls, a spirit like a small bee from "The Devil and Daniel Webster."

Now he is standing on an iron balcony. A thousand feet below him is a city with red brick houses and blue canals and railroads. Beside him on the balcony is Davy Jones. They jump off together and land on a driveway in Los Angeles. In a bungalow a wild orgy is in progress, to the tune of:

"T'aint no sin

To take off your skin
And dance around in your bones . . ."
Naked people dancing, whirling, flesh spinning off in
strips . . .

"When you hear sweet syncopation
And the music softly moans
T'aint no sin
To take off your skin
And dance around in your bones . . ."
FASTER FASTER ROUND AND ROUND

His father points to Betelgeuse in the night sky as he spins
into space beyond the shuddering Bear . . . A cliff over the city of
Lima . . . he soars over a beach where naked boys with rose genitals turn, mocking him off . . . flash of sun on water, palm trees, a
little muted schoolboy voice . . .

"The end is not Southern Boulevard on Shining Peninsula."

He is lying on a beach, gasping for breath, Davy Jones beside
him. The Antilles, 1845 . . . He looks around—the other boys are
there. Weak and emaciated, they can hardly move. Someone
holds a coconut to his mouth and he drinks the milk. Now he is
on a stretcher . . . spectral smell of vomit, a hospital room . . .

A week later the boys are recovered, lying on the beach in
their island paradise . . .

"I say just sit it out."

"Yeah why stick our neck out?"

Old Sarge: "You jokers remind me of the old Jew in the Jew
joke . . . The ship is sinking and the purser knocks on his door.
'Mr. Solomon . . . THE SHIP IS SINKING.' 'Oh vot do ve care ve don't
own the ship.'

Now look, you are in past time. You see this air line leading
to present time?"

"But Sarge we're changing the whole course of history. It
won't happen like that now."

"They still have enough atom bombs in present time to blow us out of past time. They got a hundred years saved up even if we murder Einstein in his cradle before he can pull a Moses-in-the-bulrushes . . ."

*I been working
on the railroad
All the livelong day*

Thursday, Mary Celeste 9, 1970

A hundred years ago the cobblestone street ends here. There is a little gully and some trees. Audrey is with Peter Webber and they both can fly about thirty feet in the air above the small trees.

Audrey is walking back to his father's house, a big square house on a hill. At the second floor a balcony runs across the front of the house. He finds his father in the second floor room he uses a a studio, some canvases on the wall, landscapes mostly. He tells his father how he can fly. His father looks sad and says: "We have no such powers my son."

They go out onto the balcony. The sun is setting, and a twi-

light like blue dust is settling into the valley below them which
stretches to a railroad by the sea. The Mary Celeste and the Copenhagen sail slowly by. The train passes, whistle blowing. In the
open cabin of the locomotive, two Negro firemen pound each
other on the back. The boy's face lights up in a smile as he waves
to the train. It is all a bit creaky and papier mâché but it is the best
his father can do.

He made a spattering movement with his fingers and I felt a
shower of little pebbles of light strike my hand, run up my arm
and over my body in a soft electric glow. A section of the basement was partitioned off. He opened a door.
"Sometimes I sleep in here."

My ice skates on the wall cold lost marbles in the room car-
nations three ampules of morphine.

The Chinese cook unhurried and old and nothing caring. The
Frisco Kid pale and remote.

October 15, 1972. On the way to the Angus Steak House, as
we were passing through St. James Square, John B. found the cap
of a gasoline tank still smelling of gasoline, reminding me of an
unwritten section I had planned for The Wild Boys in which the
Dead Child kills a CIA man by loosening the cap on his gas
tank—brush fires by a bumpy road.

It was a small room, the floor covered with blue linoleum,
the walls of yellow pine sanded and oiled. There was a bed with

pine bedstead, a table, a brass lamp, and some books in a pine bookcase built into the wall . . . *The Book of Knowledge,* Stevenson, *Moby Dick,* some copies of *Amazing Stories* and *Weird Tales.* Two pictures on the wall; one showing a wolf howling in a winter landscape was called The Lone Wolf. The other showed a sled pursued by a pack of wolves. In the sled was a woman in furs and a servant firing a long-barrelled pistol at the wolves as the driver whipped the horses on.

Shadows under a railroad bridge morning doves calling in the distance over the little creek the egg bursts spattering our smell of nothing that burns to the bone in puffs of window sky flowers moss.

"Have you met the Skipper yet?"

Rundown hacienda in Mexico mountain stronghold of the once powerful De Carson family. Tio Mate the family pistolero has been summoned by the young Don. "Take care of the so inconvenient Vestiori family and smile only when absolutely convenient."

"They should throw the woman out," I said and jumped because it seemed to come out without my thinking about it.

"They will if you tell them to. All you have to do is say *the* word."

Tio Mate smiles.

The spoor smell sharper red musky hair in the wind postcard

town fading into the blue shadow of a boulder across the ruined courtyard Le Comte emitted a sharp cold bray of laughter.

After the deaths of his father and mother in an epidemic of scarlet fever, Jerry Tyler ran away to join the circus. Jostled by the crowd he found himself in an eddy by a cart on which was a billboard showing a knife thrower outlining a boy in knives. A young Mexican got up from the steps of the cart. He was about twenty, dressed in khaki pants and shirt and leather moccasins.

"You crazy or something walk around alone?"

He stepped closer and put his hands on Jerry's shoulders and looked him up and down with a knowing smile. Jerry blushed and felt the blood rush to his crotch.

The Mexican looked down at his pants sticking out now at the fly. "Your thing like jellyfish chico. Need shell. Adentro."

"Survivors have learned this kindergarten lesson. They could be valuable."

He was lighting a kerosene heater. Then he lit some incense and pulled a red curtain with roses on it across the little window. He turned and looked at me and I felt the soft tingle in my crotch and I was getting hard again.

"Let's take off our clothes."

"Sure."

We sat down on the bed and took off our shoes. There were wooden pegs in the wall. We stepped over to these pegs and took off our jackets and sweat shirts. We dropped our pants and shorts and stepped out of them facing each other both hard and I saw that his was just like mine and felt a drop of pearl squeeze out the tip and at the same time a drop squeezed out the tip of his. I could

see through it like a lens that the tip was a little open the way it is
when you are really hot.

The scrotal egg hatched. A baby has died passport line. We
came to a valley where white flowers stretched away to the blue
land rising far away and I walked in a blue haze picking the flowers the heavy ferns and trees and swollen plants all around and
always water and frogs and there was an evil thing in the water
that ate our fish and a boy swimming disappeared and one night I
saw it come to the surface with its claws and a blind nose feeling
around for my scent waving in the air and I ran away from the
water then it was some time after that that the cold started.

He guided Jerry up the steps and opened the door to the cart.
Jerry stepped in and the Mexican closed the door, sliding in place
a bar across the door which was covered with heavy steel plates. It
was a long narrow room with a washstand, clothes on pegs, a
trunk, a wood stove. At one end was a wooden target with knives
sticking in it.
    The Mexican flicked Jerry's shirt. "Desnúdate chico . . .
naked . . ."
    Trembling, Jerry stripped off his clothes. The Mexican un-
dressed with quick precise movements. Jerry was gasping, choking, his whole body bright red, his heart pounding. The Mexican
guided him to the bed and laid him down on his back with a pillow under his buttocks and shoved his legs up and apart. Jerry
sighed deeply and his rectum opened like a pink mollusc.

Looking into the skull he sees a spear of stars across the sky
. . . a lance can also be a *lack,* an *absence* . . . hummm yes in the
presence of in the absence of . . . If we could cut off the supply of
uh male issue?

Then he said he had news for me and he pulled out a piece of paper and held it up so I could see it was my Mexican birth certificate. Then he tore it up and looked at me and his face got all black and ugly. I was looking beyond him at brush fires along the road.

We moved forward and put the tips together and something ran through me like soft liquid fire. He pressed me against him and kissed me on the mouth. Then he slid a hand down my backbone, feeling the joints, down between my cheeks, and put his middle finger against my ass rubbing it slowly up and down and I could feel the basement toilets and outhouses in winter and the time I did it in the woods squatting down and I saw a swampy estuary in a flash to a summer sky.

Pretty little blue-eyed teenager.

Pass it on flesh and bones withheld too long crap's last map . . . lake a canoe rose tornado in the harvest tropical jeers from Panama City.

Slowly the Mexican penetrated him and Jerry squirmed finally up against his stomach pulling his cock all the way in like liquid pink gelatin he wrapped himself around the Mexican sinking into him gasping choking as they both ejaculated his face seemed to float on the pink writhing octopus of his body contracting turning inside out in pearly spasms. Finally he went limp in the Mexican's arms the soft gelatinous clutch slowly relaxing as the boy fell asleep his red hair matted with sweat. The Mexican got up and sat on a white chair, rolled a griefa cigarette as he studied the sleeping boy and his eyes narrowed in calculation. As he watched, the boy was getting younger. Suddenly he smiled and opened his eyes. He looked about twelve. The Mexican lit the cigarette and lay down beside him with an arm around his shoulders and passed him the cigarette. Jerry inhaled and coughed. Soon he was giggling uncontrollably.

"You know what? I can write with my toes." He raised his leg and flexed his toes.

"Could you throw knives with your toes?"

"Maybe. Give me a knife."

A sweet musky smell drifts from the skull, a nitrous ozone smell, a musty dry smell of deserted outhouses and empty locker rooms.

"I want to cornhole you Peter. Know what that means?"

I nodded. I knew. It happened at the end of last summer. He was the son of a carp fisherman. They were only there in the summer to catch the great carp, some of which reached a weight of fifty pounds. There was a rumor that the carp were tinned and sold as salmon. I had often tried to catch carp using a dough bait, but never succeeded in hooking one. The boy was thin and dark, with pimples and a wide mouth with buck teeth. He lived in a little white frame house just opposite the breakwater.

The Mexican got three knives from the wooden target and placed them on the bed at Jerry's feet. Jerry propped himself up and looked at the knives measuring the distance to the target. He was getting an erection. Now he grasped a knife between his toes holding it tilted back. With a fluid movement he straightened his leg and the knife thudded into the wood. He threw two more like that and they all stuck.

"Now fuck me again."

"Listen you little pansy shit you want to go back to a reformatory? You want to get gang fucked till your asshole splits open? HUH?"

Tio Mate smiles.

"Fuck me up the ass."
Buck teeth he lived in a little white frame house just opposite the breakwater. He got some vaseline from a drawer down on his stomach legs spread I straddled him looking at his ass rubbing it slow pants squirming toilets and outhouses squeezed inside me.
"I want to cornhole you Peter."
He sighed and squirmed really hot spread my legs sweat quivering what that means down on the bed on my stomach.

The Mexican began to tickle him and Jerry laughed until he pissed, twisting over the side of the bed. The Mexican pulled him off the bed and bent him over the white chair. He put a throwing knife into the boy's hand.
"Throw it when you go off."
As the boy ejaculated, the Mexican pulled him up straight with a hand across his stomach. With a sharp animal cry Jerry threw a knife straight into the bullseye.
So Jerry joined the circus as the knife thrower's second. The Mexican taught him how to fight with a knife and with his bare hands, and he got over his fear of physical combat.

The boys are summoned before the skull and their training begins. The smell of the skull on first exposure precipitates sexual frenzies. The boys tear off their clothes ejaculating, the red skull rash burning in lips and nipples crotch and rectum as the skull smell steams off their bodies. They will learn to draw, aim and fire in the moment of orgasm, to throw a knife and use rifle and tommy gun. They will learn to conceive plans in this moment. They will learn that *sex is power.*

I had already decided what to do but I decided to be vague or he would get suspicious . . . he was like that, he could see people's minds.

Whole body inside me squirming towards the surface and suddenly there was a flash of light behind my eyes and he was all the way in his face in mine and his cock touching the end of mine and I went off in blue flashes of light. I was standing now above the bed and looking around the room and saw the wolf picture had come alive. As I watched, the servant and his son suddenly grabbed the woman, stripped off her fur coat and threw her screaming out of the sled. The boy put on the coat and I was him now, feeling the coat around my body and watching the circle of wolves around the woman back there in the bloody snow.

Ali waits. Long overdue.

Let the wind blow through you a field lightness in my legs through the field across the cold blue Michigan sky summer in my crotch I was getting hard the door opened and turned around to face him sticking out at the fly my body was blowing away wooden fence with a gate.

CIA agent faded in the mirror. Ali at the door. Blue stars in the sky.

"Go there soon?"

Meet Me in St. Louis Louie

Audrey Carsons at sixteen was in many ways older than his years. He already possessed the writer's self-knowledge and self-disgust, and the God-guilt all writers feel in creation. In other ways he was younger than sixteen. He was sadly lacking in social graces and worldly experience. He could not dance, play games, or make light conversation. He was painfully shy, his knowledge of sex culled from *Coming of Age in Samoa* and a book entitled *Sex and Marriage*. His face was scarred with festering spiritual wounds, and there was no youth in it. At the same time he was compulsively infantile. The combination was not pleasing when compounded with sick self-disgust, fear, and impotent rage. He had the look of a desperate and thoroughly unsuccessful black magician caught out with cards raining from his sleeve. There was a horrible unknown odor about him of a frozen mummy thawing out in a fetid swamp.

"You are a walking corpse," Mrs. Greenfield told him indirectly through a friend who she knew would repeat her verdict. It was a way she had. Years later when he heard she had died, Audrey got his back. It's a way writers have.

"It isn't every corpse that can walk."

"He looks like a sheep-killing dog," snapped Colonel Greenfield, a fine old whitey with a clipped grey mustache.

Audrey got his back there too, when he heard about the colonel's death from a massive hemorrhage.

"I *am* a sheep-killing dog."

The mills of a writer grind slowly but they grind exceeding fine. He felt himself locked up somewhere in a dingy attic, watching helplessly while shopkeepers shoved his change back at him without a thank you. Bartenders took one look at that face and said:

"We don't want your type in here."

These slights cut his raw wounds like rock salt. He felt that nobody wanted his type anywhere. He read *Adventure* magazine and dreamed of himself in sun helmet and khakis, a Webley at his belt, his faithful Zulu servant at his side. These dreams were banal and childish even for his years, consisting mostly of gunfights at which he excelled. Since adventure was a virtual impossibility in a midwestern matriarchy, these were paper-thin dreams, 19th century nostalgia. What he hoped for most of all was to escape from his tainted flesh through some heroic act.

He was the only scholarship boy at an exclusive school known as the Poindexter Academy. Audrey read *Adventure Stories* and *Short Stories* and saw himself as the Major, a gentleman adventurer and IDB (Illegal Diamond Buyer) . . . in a good cause, that is. He read *Amazing Stories* and saw himself as the first man to land on the moon and drew diagrams of rocket ships. He decided to be a writer and make his own Majors and Zulu Jims

and Snowy Joes and Carl Cranberrys. His first literary composi-
tion, "The Autobiography of a Wolf", was inspired by a book called
The Biography of a Grizzly Bear . . . Feeling the snow under
his feet; his blazing eyes; his fangs; and licking the blood off the
face of his wolf mate Jerry. Audrey was a little vague about the
sexes, and saw no reason why he couldn't take Jerry, a red-haired
wolf, as his mate. Later he took on another mate, a delicate albino
wolf with blue eyes who froze to death in a blizzard. Whitey had
always been a delicate wolf. When Jerry dies of consumption,
spitting blood into the snow, Audrey is so weakened by grief that
he is attacked and eaten by the grizzly bear as a punishment for
plagiarism.

His family were in very modest circumstances. It humiliated
him to attend classes in his patched blue suit—shabby patches,
not the splendid leather things on the elbows of a worn Brooks
Brother jacket. He was invited to some of the parties, and some of
the mothers tried to put him at ease. "That nice quiet Carsons
boy," said Mrs. Kindheart. Her kindness was of course the kiss of
death, under the cold eyes of Mrs. Worldly.

The hero of his stories was a young aristocrat lounging dis-
dainfully at the wheel of his Stutz Bearcat, exercising a *droit de
seigneur* over provincial debutantes of St. Louis. As it turned out
he had underworld connections, was perhaps involved in illegal
diamond buying, white slavery or the opium traffic. At the opening of the Academy in mid-September, such a hero did indeed appear. Aloof and mysterious, where he came from nobody knew.
Audrey thought of him as the man Flamonde in the poem by Ed-
ward Arlington Robinson:

> *The man Flamonde from God knows where*
> *With firm address and foreign air*

There were rumors of Tangier, Paris, London, New York, a
school in Switzerland where the boys took drugs. His name was
John Hamlin and he lived with relatives in a huge marble house in

Portland Place. He drove a magnificent Duesenberg. Audrey wrote: "Clearly he has come a long way. Travel-stained and even the stains unfamiliar, cuff links of a strange dull metal that seems to *absorb* light, large green eyes well apart, his red hair touched with gold, a straight nose, a beautiful cupid's bow mouth . . ." He scratched out "beautiful"—too fruity he thought—and substituted "perfect". And the new boy took a liking to Audrey, while he turned aside invitations from sons of the rich.

"They bore me," he told Audrey, who flushed with pleasure. He was flattered and flustered by Hamlin's attention. He would come home blushing to remember the agonized stammerings and attempts to be clever that didn't quite come off, convinced that Hamlin must despise him. But Hamlin remained friendly in his detached way. And Audrey continued to peck away at his typewriter, amending his lame conversation with the New Boy until it sparkled with epigrams.

It was Tuesday afternoon, October 23, 1928—a clear bright day, leaves falling. October's bright blue weather. Audrey walked up Pershing Avenue to the corner of Walton. He was thinking about a story he was writing with John Hamlin as the hero. It was a ghost story about a mysterious encounter in Harbor Beach where his family spent the summers.

"I could never find the cottage again. But once I described the boy to my father, who said yes, there had been a John Hamlin among the summer people, but he was killed in an auto accident outside St. Louis."

Right at his elbow the calm voice: "Hello Audrey. Like to take a ride?" And there was Hamlin at the wheel of his Duesenberg. He opened the door without waiting for an answer. Audrey got in. Hamlin shifted gears and the Duesenberg shot forward, slamming the door. Right turn on Taylor—the trees and red brick of the Catholic school flashed by and Audrey glimpsed the gold dome of the cathedral glittering in cold sunlight. Right on Lindell Boulevard heading west, houses and trees a blur of red and green

and yellow as the Duesenberg gathered speed. Skinner . . . city
limits. The streets were oddly empty.

Hamlin was silent, his eyes fixed on the road. Outside Clayton he pressed the accelerator to the floor. The car seemed to
leave the ground in a swirl of dead leaves. Audrey must have
dozed. The car was moving slowly over a dirt road, but what he
saw bore no resemblance to the Missouri countryside. It looked
flat and dusty and there were people by the side of the road
dressed in white robes. Suddenly six young boys naked except for
colored jock straps barred . . .

Meet Me at the Fair

... the way. The leader was carrying a Mauser pistol clipped onto a rifle stock. Audrey recognized this weapon from the Stoeger catalogue, *The Shooter's Bible,* which he read religiously, studying each weapon and deciding which ones he wanted to carry when he became a gentleman adventurer. He knew the caliber of this gun, nine millimeter, but not the same cartridge as the Luger. He knew that the wooden stock also served as a holster; that the magazine, which was not in the handle but in front of the handle, also served as a hand hold to steady the weapon; that the magazine held nine cartridges. The leader stepped to the side of the car. Hamlin spoke briefly in a language unknown to Audrey and the leader nodded.

"We leave the car here," John said.

Audrey got out. They were on the edge of what looked like a vast fair—booths and lights as far as Audrey could see in a sepia twilight. He decided that the nonchalant thing was to ask no questions. He followed John through the square where a number of acts were in progress, each surrounded by a circle of onlookers. He glimpsed these acts out of the corner of his eye, for John was walking rapidly as if he had an appointment to keep.

"For I have promises to keep and miles to go before I sleep," Audrey recited inanely to himself.

In one circle two boys were practising Jiu Jitsu. Audrey had once ordered a book on jiu jitsu through a mail order firm in Wisconsin. He found the instructions and diagrams quite incomprehensible . . . 'Seize your opponent by his right sleeve with your left hand and pull sharply downwards while your right hand secures his left lapel. At the same time move your left foot quickly behind his right heel. Straighten your body with a twist to the right. He will be thrown heavily to the ground.' As he watched, one of the boys fell backward with a foot in the other's stomach. He straightened his leg, every muscle outlined like marble in the dying sun, and the boy sailed over the heads of the onlookers and lit on his feet like a cat.

Other acts were enigmatic. In one circle boys were dressing and undressing at prestidiginal speed. He passed a circle where a strange woolly monkey was attacking a dummy with a knife while the trainer stood behind him giving inaudible signals. There were no noisy children about, and no families. The people he passed were dressed in colored jock straps, leather jock straps, knee length shorts, and Arab robes. Most of them seemed to be adolescent, with a sprinkling of older people. A white-haired man passed in a fiacre. Around the square were lodging houses, cafes, Turkish baths and boardwalks. He caught a whiff of the sea. Streets and alleys opened off the square. Boys lounged in doorways.

As he walked along, Audrey glimpsed scenes that sent the

blood singing in his ears and pounding to his crotch. Why, some of the boys were *out of control* (Audrey's term for erection) and *doing things together.* He could feel the pull in his groin. John had turned into a weed-grown cobblestone street—blue twilight and trees ahead—this looked like St. Louis again. Here comes the old lamplighter. Ah here we are. Red brick house on the corner. The lawn was weed-grown and there were leaves on the cracked sidewalk. John opened a side door under a portico.

"My father's house. Enter."

Dark stairs to the top floor. John opened a door and turned on the light. It was an attic room with a double brass bed, a washstand, a copper lustre basin and pitcher. Audrey saw some sepia prints on the wall that seemed to represent the fair they had just walked through. There was a bookcase with leatherbound gilt-edged books. John took off his jacket, tie and shirt, poured water into the basin, and washed his face and neck. He dried himself with a blue towel, sat down on the edge of the bed and took off his shoes and socks.

He lay down on the bed with his knees up and pillows behind his head, selected an orange from a basket of fruit on the night table. He peeled the orange and the smell of oranges filled the room. He ate the orange, spilling juice on his naked chest. Audrey was washing with his shirt on, the collar turned back.

"Toss me that wash rag, Audrey."

John wiped the orange juice off his chest and licked his fingers. He lit a cigarette and looked at Audrey through the smoke.

"I want to see you stripped, Audrey."

Cold in the stomach untying his shoes shoes falling to the floor pants folded on the chair. He stood up.

"Take off your shorts too."

They caught in a way that made him uncomfortable fell to his ankles he kicked them onto a chair his nakedness John's hand rubbing lubricant and the silver sparks went off behind his eyes. His head exploded in pictures. It seemed that he had lived in this room for a long time a ceiling crossed by car lights from the street and the opening and closing of doors these stairs . . .

"You know both of us use the copper lustre basin in the attic room now Johnny's back."

Drifting sand, fish smells and dead eyes in doorways, shabby quarters of a forgotten city. I was beginning to remember the pawn shops, guns and brass knucks in a window, chili parlors, cheap rooming houses, a cold wind from the sea. Dead eyes seemed to be looking at some distant beginning to remember the boy, an old skating rink . . . any minute now . . . Who said Atlantic City? . . . wire rusty around jagged holes . . . Van's Surgery . . . writing croaker . . . Globe Hotel . . . Great Atlantic Accident . . . name address hotel quite right? . . . a number . . . police line ahead frisking seven boys against a wall. Too late to turn back, they'd seen us. And then I saw the photographers, more photographers than a routine frisk would draw. I eased a film grenade into my hand. A cop stepped toward us. I pushed the plunger down and brought my hands up, tossing the grenade into the air. A black explosion blotted out the set and we were running down a dark street toward the barrier. Behind us the city went up in chunks.

GREAT ATLANTIC ACCIDENT . . . READ ALL ABOUT IT.

We ran on and burst out of a black silver mist into late afternoon sunlight on a suburban street, cracked pavements, sharp smell of weeds.

"Roller skate boys very close now." The Dib touched pillars and posts as he walked. He pointed to a stucco building that occupied half a block. "There, in old skating rink."

The rink was boarded up and looked deserted from the outside. The Dib knocked on a side door, which opened silently on oiled hinges. In the doorway stood a tall blond youth in a blue jock strap. He carried a machine pistol under one arm. He looked at me with metallic grey eyes.

"Come in," he said and stepped aside.

I looked around for the Dib. He had disappeared. "He's gone."

"*Naturlich.* It is his work."

In the middle of the rink some boys in blue jock straps were skating. Sunlight poured through a broken skylight of wired glass. The wire was rusty around jagged holes, made I would guess by grenades or mortars. Mattresses here and there, boys sat naked smoking hashish and drinking tea, a work bench along one wall where boys were sharpening knives, oiling skates, repairing bicycles, a long bicycle rack by the work bench. On a mat four boys were practicing judo and karate. Others threw knives into a target. Scene from a silent film. No laughing no shouting no horse play. Boys turned to look at me as I passed, faces unsmiling, eyes cool and watchful. All movements were purposeful and controlled. No boy was fidgeting or standing aimlessly around. The boy with the pistol took me to what had been the office of the rink. It was fitted out as a ward room, maps on the wall, pins in the maps.

"Do you have any ammunition?" he asked me.

I put a box of fifty shells on the table.

"We must distribute these. We have five .38 police revolvers here." He handed me five shells.

He stepped to the door and spoke in the language. A thin dark boy, face spattered with adolescent pimples, came over from the work bench. He was naked except for a blue jock strap. He motioned for me to follow. Dusty window boarded up, boys at a table peeling potatoes and cutting meat. He slid behind a counter where the skates had once been issued to noisy teenage patrons. He measured me with his eyes and dumped some clothes on the counter—sweat shirts, blue jeans, blue jock straps, socks. He passed me a bowie knife 18 inches long with a worn black belt and sheath. I hefted the knife in my hands. The handle was a knuckle duster that ended in a brass knob. It was a beautifully balanced fighting instrument honed to razor sharpness.

"Just take any locker empty and change," he told me.

I stashed my clothes in a locker and changed into blue jeans and sweat shirt.

"You want to be measured for skates and crash helmet and bucklers."

The cobbler was an old man in a dusty room, tools and leather laid out on a long table. He looked at me from eyes faded as pale sky. Unhurried and old, he measured my feet, head and forearms. The boy leaned against the door jamb watching. The cobbler completed his measurements and nodded.

"Bath?" the boy asked. Walking behind him I spotted a pimple where his naked buttocks rubbed together and another on the left cheek. He felt my eyes, stopped and turned to look at me over his shoulder. I touched the pimples with my finger tips, caressing his buttocks. He moved slightly and rubbed his jock strap dusty windows boarded up wooden benches smell of sweat and mouldy jock straps several boys changing. The boy sat down on a bench and pulled his jock strap down, tossing it into a locker. He had a half erection. He looked down as his cock got stiff.

"You strip."

I pulled off my clothes. He looked at me with unsmiling appraisal. "You fuck me this time," he decided.

He led the way through a green door. A shower room with white tile floor had been fitted out as a haman. A youth had just poured a bucket of water over himself. He turned with an erection, shook water from his eyes, measuring me with his thin brown body. He reached out a slow foot and brought it down my calf and said something to the dark boy. Three youths sat on a bench comparing erections. The boy filled a bucket, poured half of it over me and the rest on himself. We passed a piece of carbolic soap back and forth. One of the youths tossed us a towel and we dried our bodies. There was a tube of KY on a shelf. I picked it up.

The boy leaned forward holding his cheeks apart. I touched his pimples then rubbed the lubricant on his ass and up inside the ring squeezing my finger hitched hands around his hips and pulled him towards me feeling the spasmodic milking movements as I slid it in and out the electric warmth of his quivering body. The other youths stood around us watching silently and at the climax let out a little sigh from parted lips. We walked out naked into the rink.

It was late afternoon and the sides of the rink were in shadow. Some of the boys were cooking and making tea. Others were engaged in group sexual exercises. A circle of boys sat on the karate mat looking at each other's genitals in silent concentration. Now one of the boys was getting stiff. He walked to the center of the circle, turned around three times and sat down hugging his knees. He looked from one face to the other. His eyes locked with one boy and a current passed between them. There was a click as if a picture had been taken. The boy in the center of the circle opened his legs and lay back with his head on a leather cushion. A drop of lubricant squeezed out the end of his phallus as he arched his body and squirmed. The boy selected kneeled in front of the other studying his genitals. He pressed the tip open and looked at it through a lens of lubricant. He twisted the tight nuts gently with precise fingers as if he were tuning up a piece of machinery, handling the phallus as a precision instrument, running a slow finger up and down the shaft, rubbing lubricant along the divide line, feeling for sensitive spots in the tip. The circle of boys sat silent, lips parted, watching faces there calmed to razor sharpness. The boy who was being masturbated rocked back hugging knees against his chest. Quivering in an ecstasy of exposure his body blurred out of focus. He lay there unconscious. Two boys carried him to a mattress and covered his body with a blue blanket. Another boy took his place in the center of the circle.

I was tired and hungry. Some boys motioned me to sit down, handed me a plate of stew and a wedge of dark Arab bread. After eating I found a mattress and fell asleep. When I woke up the rink was full of yellow grey light. A boy was leaning on his elbow looking at me. It was the boy who had touched me with his foot in the bath. Our eyes met. There was a click in my head a melting of the stomach on hands and knees a band squeezing my head tighter tighter taste of metal in the mouth. I was looking down from the ceiling then out through the broken skylight turning figure eights in the morning sky.

There are about thirty boys here of all races and nationalities: Negroes, Chinese, Mexicans, Arabs, Danes, Swedes, Americans, English. That is, they are evidently derived from racial and national stock corresponding to Negroes, Mexicans, Danes, Americans et cetera. However, these boys are a new breed.

After a breakfast of bread and tea, six boys put on jock straps, crash helmets and skates and buckled on their knives in preparation for a reconnaisance patrol. The blond boy with the machine pistol will accompany them as patrol leader. Others are busy at the work benches, sharpening knives, oiling skates, fixing bicycles, improvising weapons. One weapon works on the crossbow principle with strong rubber bands instead of a bow. Lead slugs are fed in from a magazine on top of the weapon and drop into a slot when the gun is cocked by pulling the bands back. The rifle models are amazingly accurate up to twenty yards and the slugs embed themselves in soft wood. A murderous bolo is made by attaching lead weights to each end of a bicycle chain. The boys practice continually with these devices.

The pimply boy approaches with a folder under his arm, wearing blue jeans. He looks like an American school boy except for the cool eyes alert and disengaged. He addresses me in a curiously unaccented English.

"I teach you picture language," he taps folder. "No good talk old language." He clears a space on the work bench and opens the folder. The written language is a simplified script obviously derived from the Egyptian. The pictures are then transliterated into verbal units. Any picture can be said in a number of ways according to the context. For five days, we study ten hours a day. My previous study of Egyptian hieroglyphs greatly facilitates my progress and I am now able to converse with some ease. Pictures rise out of the words. I am learning something of the history and customs of the wild boys. Once a year all the wild boys meet in one spot to compare weapons and fighting techniques and to indulge in communal orgies. This festival is known as Xolotl Time.

"Many different boy some almost like fish live all time in water since he begin."

I ask what he means by begin—since birth?

"Wild boy not born now. First he made from little piece one boy's ass grow new boy. Piece cut from boy after he get fucked. Boy like much get fucked give best piece. Grow new boy then boy give piece take new one back his tribe. Boy grow like this not like boy born no good cunt. Boy grow from piece change many different way. Some boy no talk make pictures in head. Boy make cry kill man over there there." He points across the rink. "Other got electricity in body. Boy live far south warm wet place very sweet very rotten inside. Dress up like woman kill many soldier." (These boys who are called "Bubus" secrete a substance from the rectum and genitals which leaves erogenous sores rotting flesh to the bone.) "You scratch feel good scratch more pretty soon scratch self away jump around in your bones. Some boy he glow in dark. You come near soon die. You come near little bit every day you all right. Very good for fuck. Him very hot inside. Other boy he look you come off in pants." And the dreaded "laughing boys": "You laugh too piss self laugh guts out." (The "laughing boys" also communicate fatal fits of sneezing, coughing and hiccuping.) "Other live blue place in mountains got little high blue note you hear that you need all time you hooked. Boy got poison teeth like snake. Lizard boy live on cliffs hand so strong crush bones." The boys with built-in weapons are known as biologics. Other of more or less normal physical attributes specialize in the use of some skill or weapon . . . glider boys, knife throwers, bowmen, sling-shot boys, blow-gun boys. "Got darts all different size some so small you think mosquito bites you then turn blue and die." One tribe specializes in musical weapons. "Got music so sweet man walk over cliff. Make sound knock down wall shake guts out."

"Many boy tribe come Xolotl Time all different every time more different. Not need take piece now. We make Zimbu boy. Make many Zimbu Xolotl Time." I ask when this festival occurs. "Different time place every year. I think this time in south on sea maybe not know for sure till two weeks before time all boy stop fuck jack off he get there hot like fire."

The spoken language has great flexibility and extraordinary vividness through immediate pictorial association. If you can't see it you can't say it. As to the origins of this language, the boy is vague. "Wild boys written long time ago in picture book. Book called 'breathing book.' One man come show us piece from book." The wild boys have no sense of time and date the beginning from 1969 when the first wild boy groups were formed.

I now have my skates, crash helmet, and leather bucklers for the forearms, all perfectly tailored like extensions of my body. The skate rollers can be locked and rubber caps adjusted for walking uphill. Tomorrow I will go on patrol. Patrols consist of six boys on skates and one boy on a bicycle. The bicycle boy is the patrol leader. This job rotates and leadership is informal. It is his job to coordinate the activities of the patrol and the information gathered. He carries a pistol and field glasses in addition to the standard bowie knife.

We set out at dawn through ruined suburbs, a crescent moon in the china blue morning sky. The patrol leader is a tall thin Negro boy, ears flat against his small head, a distant savannah in his eyes. The boys are skating in a line, hands on each other's shoulders. We come to an intersection of subdivision streets which forms a wide expanse of cracked weed-grown pavement. The leader rides ahead to the top of a steep hill on his bicycle and scans the surrounding country through field glasses. He comes back and says one word which means empty land to sky. A boy rubs his jock strap and with one accord the boys sit down pulling their jock straps down over their skates. They skate on slow circles touching each other's genitals and buttocks as they pass.

A boy skates up behind me, puts his hand on my shoulder and guides me to a broken wall. Three of us brace ourselves against the wall then we are twisting in circles spinning the moon and the sky throwing sperm across the cracked pavements.

In the late afternoon we pass a ruined building. US Consulate. On a windy hillside we sight a herd of goats. The goatherd waves and runs towards us, wind whipping his torn djellaba. Young actor is about thirteen. He tells us a truckload of American soldiers passed the Consulate this morning and asked him where the wild boys were hiding.

"Americans very bor bor. Give me cigarettes, chocolate, corned bif. Believe everything what I say."

He takes a stick and draws a map to show the false route he has given them. The leader studies the map, sketches it on a clip board, pointing and asking questions. Satisfied that the map is accurate, he hands the boy a piece of hashish and a switch knife. The boy snaps the knife open and cuts the air. "One day kill son bitch Merican."

I put my hand on the back of the boy's neck. He moves eagerly under my hands like a dog, squirms out of his djellaba and stands naked in the wind, pubic hairs blown flat against his groin. He arches his body as I jack him off . . . the wind spatters sperm across his lean brown stomach.

That night we decide on an ambush plan for the truck. Our undercover agents working as cooks, bus boys, waiters, bartenders have administered Bor Bor to the American troops. The effect of this drug, which is held in horror by the wild boys and only used as a weapon against our enemies, is to lull the user into a state of fuzzy well-being and benevolence, a warm good feeling that everything will come out all right for Americans.

"We like apple pie and we like each other, it's just as simple as that."

Jolting along in the truck . . . "Oh God, isn't mother a grand person? She's got all the good qualities . . ." Muttering squirming bursting into maudlin song:

"Your mother and mine . . ."

"With a heart that was willing to share . . ."

"Let me bang her twice a month and what could be fairer than that unless it's our old Colonel. When I die I want to be buried right in the same coffin with that fine old blue-eyed whitey— always putting his hands on our shoulders and calls us Son and weeps like a baby over the dead and wounded. He was an Eagle Scout at birth."

A truckload of tough soldiers, crooning, singing, weeping, muttering, smiling, squirming around like randy dogs under Massa's kind old hands. A Sea Org member of Scientology leaps up and screams out: "THANK YOU RON THANK YOU RON THANK YOU RON! . . ."

Another soldier throws his arms around the Jew from Brooklyn . . .

"You Jews is so warm and human!"

Another sobs out: "All the darkies is a-weepin' cause Massa's in the cold cold grave . . ." As he buries a good Darky and a dead dog . . .

"Cried like babies right in front of each other—'why be ashamed to show your heart son' said a wise old whisky priest and I sobbed in that good man's arms and the cop threw his great paws around both of us and we cried all over each other."

Mother and Old Glory, kindly priests, good cops, adorable prison wardens rocked in the arms of Bor Bor . . .

A thin sliver of moon in the blue black sky. The cold at night

here grabs your flesh into goose pimples. We slung an iron telephone pole thirty feet long between chains, a line of boys on
skates on both sides down a steep hill, the pole pulling us along
faster and faster like a comet—hit the truck dead center and
knocked it over spilling those Bor Bor heads on the cold cold
ground. We swept around from both sides and cut them to Old
Glory and back. Under a rough cross formed by the skewered
truck we broke thin ice in a fountain and washed the blood off us.
We now have a supply of firearms for the next operation.

   The roller skate boys swerve down a wide palm-lined avenue
into a screaming blizzard of machine gun bullets . . . humming
boys, a vibration that sets the teeth on edge and rages through the
brain like buzz saws . . . messages whistled through cold alleys,
taken up by the barking of dogs, reach the remote communes in a
few hours . . . he was coming down windy streets, white shorts
slapping, mouth open, their hairs up at the first ripple whimper
off putrid sweet legs throw back their heads and howl the winds
ass hairs erectile—plant boys who know the weeds and vines,
marijuana behind enemy lines, hay fever on the wind, water hyacinths snarl the boat propellor, marijuana sprouts by the barracks,
thorns scratch the Colonel's boots, boys who can call the locusts
and fleas, beautiful diseased Bubu boy stands by a black lagoon,
fragile dream boys of shaded dawn wait by attic windows in a lost
street of slate roofs and brick chimneys, shaman boys the young
faces dark with death, a young red-haired soldier, his ears trembling, yelps, ejaculates strange streets dank school toilets a wind
across the golf course naked semen spurting shy spirits in a world
of shades boy touches a shoulder under the blankets gasping as
the other holds his knees back his thin buttocks his rectum wet
morning cobblestone rain in cobwebs the blue desert who exist
can breathe there tenuous rose vines bodies cool backs his little
teeth scream and yelp boys cuddle whimpering in sleep, a naked

boy with his back to Audrey rubs against another, the boy turns and grins at Audrey.

Late afternoon light I could touch the sea wall the stone the vines I could see my body and the sand the face down there a thin pale back two boys laughing blue youth in their eyes sunny the house behind him bleakly clear I am the boy as a child and this is me lying naked on his underwear rubbing himself my room and me there he smiled to watch him do it jumped across a gleaming empty sky I could feel unknown hand orange in the shed long long how long it was the skies fall apart dust of the dead in his eyes into his eggs tighter tighter then I was spurting into a ruined courtyard a smell of oats.

Back in Mexico City, the man who was the boy's father tried to raise money to come back and dig some more in the ruins, but the Mexican authorities said he had no right to do this and took what he had found away from him and sent some Mexicans to the ruins. The man began taking morphine again and I spent most of my time in the streets to stay out of the house. I remember an American from Texas with prison shadows in his eyes talked to me in the park and I went back with him to his apartment.

It was some time after that that a man came to the club and selected me as his caddy. He was a youngish man, about thirty, with very pale grey eyes . . . fat, but I could see there were muscles under the fat, and I could see that he had something special he wanted from me as soon as we got out on the golf course. First he told me I shouldn't be hanging around in Mexico, that I belonged in America because I was an American and he could arrange this but first I would have to do something he wanted me to do in order to "square myself" as he put it. Then he told me that "the free world" as he called it was fighting for its life and I could help.

There was a man they knew was working with the Commies and they wanted to get him. I'd already seen this man, he bought me a sandwich and an orange drink . . . now all I had to do was to get the man you know what I mean to start something with me and they would nail him and that would be it—after that I could go to America and live with a decent family and go to school, now how did that sound to me? I told him I was born in Mexico and didn't want to go to America, that my parents were here and I had to help them with the money I made. Then he grabbed me by the arms and I saw he had a snubnose .38 in a holster under his arm.

"All right look at me when you talk and stop lying. I know all about you. Your father is a junkie and your mother is a lush and you've been peddling your ass in the Alameda for the past year . . ."

I told him that I would do what he wanted and he showed me Mexicans wouldn't let him take me to America. Then he said he had news for me and he pulled out a piece of paper and held it up so I could see it was my Mexican birth certificate. Then he tore it up and looked at me and his face got all black and ugly. I was looking beyond him at the brush fires along the road.

"Listen you little pansy shit you want to go back to a reformatory? You want to get gang fucked till your asshole splits open? HUH? Well I can sign a court order and get you into a federal reformatory in Texas before you can fart . . ."

I told him that I would do what he wanted and he showed me a place by the pond.

"Right here where your boy friend cornholed you. That picture gets you out of parental custody . . ."

I had already decided what to do but I decided to argue or he would get suspicious—he was like that, could see people's minds—so I asked if I could stay in Mexico if I did what he wanted and he said I could if I wanted to and I knew he was lying or if I was allowed to stay he would want more such work from me but I pretended to believe him. It was set up for the day after tomorrow which would be Friday.

When I got back to the changing shed Johnny was there alone and I told him what had happened and the plan I had. As we walked out through the parking lot Johnny unscrewed the cap on the man's gas tank leaving it held by the very end of the screws so it would fly off on the first bump. We were sure to be suspected so we went to hide out with Tio Mate in Northern Mexico in a little town surrounded by opium growers. If anyone asked we were not there. We read about it in the papers the next day but the heat was not on right away as we had expected because somebody else had been there before us with an explosive device devised by the CIA itself to be attached to gas tanks. That of course sent them running after professionals or enemy agents within their ranks.

Just to Pass
the Time Away

Brad and Greg had been working on something terribly hush hush
with the space program and then they were called in and allowed
to resign without prejudice. It was all so terribly unfair—they'd
worked so hard and just because some CID creep had been nosing
around Tangiers where they took their vacations. That was three
months ago, and now they are working for a private foundation. It
all has to do with making a new person from a cutting. They have
a modern clinic and the donors will be passed along through
channels.

The first two arrived on roller skates wearing absolutely
nothing else but blue jock straps. Greg and Brad nearly swooned
at sight of them. One was a slim dark boy about sixteen, a little
pimply and that can be terribly attractive you know, and Brad

thought "My God that's me!" The other had Mongoloid features, body smooth and hard as teakwood, with two blue tattoos on each rump and Greg thought "My God that's me!"

So we take these two divine numbers to the examination room and explain we have to take a cutting from the rectum, very small and quite painless, and uh well the more *excited* they are when we cut off a piece the better chance there is the piece will *make* . . . It's all very technical—first we have to take *measurements*. They just nod matter of fact and peel off their straps and get hardons like they can *control* it. The young one stands there chewing gum while I measure him. Then we take them to one of the cutting rooms where we have tape recorders, cameras, orgone funnels and film sets.

The set for this one is a deserted gymnasium, dust in the air, a mouldy mat. The little pimply boy is down on all fours, the other just ready. I tell the tattoo to hold on while I slip a cutting tube up him. These are plastic perforated with pinpoint holes and inside is a rotary knife operated electrically; when the ring contracts it forces bits of the lining through the holes which are then clipped off by the knife. They are in all sizes and for him I use a tube no thicker than a pencil—he is very tight. The little boy spits out his gum and they start, not minding at all about Brad and me watching. As soon as the tattoo comes and I have the clipping I slap his rump and he pulls out and I take a cutting from the other boy who is still contracting and gasping. The boys take a shower in the rusty locker room and I tell them to come back Saturday. I want a solo clipping from the little boy taken just when he comes. I will use a vibrating tube just the right size from the other boy's measurements.

Saturday he comes back with his friend to watch and we arrange him on the bed with his knees up, rubber slings behind the knees attached to the wall to keep him spread, and turn an orgone funnel on his ass and balls and cock. He squirms showing his sharp teeth and when I slide it in and turn on the vibrator he blurs out of focus and comes up to his chin and I say to Brad "My God this one will *make!*"

There were a lot of boys came in like that—attractive normal looking kids. Many of them had skills they wanted to pass right along and we take cuttings of the boys doing their thing: throwing knives, shooting, gliding, skating etc.

Two Karate boys. One fuck other standing up. When he come let out KIAI shatter picture window and breaks a stack of bricks.

Two young bank robbers in pea green suits grey fedoras. Cheap hotel, money spread out on the bed. The money has excited them like catnip. They strip down lubricating and roll around in it. They cut high card to see who fucks the other. Ace of spades wins—he is fucking the other boy on all fours when the fuzz bust in, eyes popping out of their heads when they see what the boys are doing. Still stuck together, the boys snatch up two Walther automatics fitted with silencers. Hair stands up on their heads as they come SPUT SPUT SPUT sperm rectal mucus and cordite. The fuzz men go down under a hail of silent bullets.

The Circus Boys train animals for assassination and sabotage. A woolly monkey creeps into the general's tent with a little curved knife. Sophisticated martens know all the best arteries. Man-eating tigers have a taste for white meat. A whole circus camps in front of the clinic and we take cuttings while they do their acts. They know the animal wavelengths, they can turn it on or turn it off. They can panic stampede or drive them mad with rage. The boys talk in growls and snarls and purrs and yipes and show their teeth at each other like wild dogs. When they fuck they show *all* their teeth whine and whimper off you can see the hair stand up on the ankles first ripple up the legs in goose pimples even the ass hairs stand out straight up back of the neck to the crown. They throw back their heads and howl and a pack of wolves howls with them.

Pim Pam the elephant boy is five feet tall, one eye black, the other green. He never talks but he gives out vibrations you can feel *inside.* We have to take his cutting on location down where the elephants roam—a big herd about three hundred yards ahead. Several hundred naked Biafra recruits stand around and come to attention. Pim Pam bends over hands on knees and I slide a cutting tube up his thin tight ass and turn on the vibrator. He starts to tremble all over and move his head from side to side, eyes spitting panic. When he comes it jumps out of him whistles through the grass and hits the elephants. They toss their trunks in the air and stampede it shakes the ground straight for the English Consulate. I ask the boy how he does it and he writes on a slate: "I see what I want to happen and when I come it does."

1920 gun boys tommy gun black Cadillac. They strip down to Star Dust. One sits in the back seat. The gun boy squirms down on his pal—he sort of opens up—you can feel the pull in his nuts tearing through empty streets lips drawn back eyes shiny. There they are on a corner, three guns from the West Side. He pivots around jissom empty shells raining on his body cuts them down.

The Shaman Boys do acts to make the enemy sneeze and laugh and hiccup. Two of them fuck standing up, begin to laugh and laugh, laughing out the spurts and the laugh jumps right inside you. Fuck on all fours then they rear up on their knees and both of them spray it out ACHOO ACHOO ACHOO—they can throw it fifty feet. One squirms down on another's lap and they both start to hiccup slow at first then fast faster spitting the hiccups out like bullets. Other boys can bring wind and earthquakes naked on a hill knee deep in grass hips moving slow throw up their arms "Wind Wind Wind" and the wind rises whistling around their bodies blows the sperm back. And then the hurricane hits. The Seismic Boys fuck slow and heavy seventy tons to the square inch you can feel it build up under the earth's crust houses falling people running the boys scream and rumble and shake their hips as crevices open up in the ground.

Music Boys with flutes and drums and zithers, intricate webs of wool and strings and wires that draw music from the wind. Yellow-haired boy wolfish Pan face blue eyes spread in the sling a black boy squats between his knees and shoves the vibrator in. The Pan boy plays the flute faster and faster and when he comes it throws Brad and me to the floor. It is PANIC. A boy black and shiny as obsidian kneels with the drum between his legs, another behind him working it in and out to drum beats. The boys dance a naked figure eight to the pounding drums, leave one boy standing in the center. He is a mixture of Chinese and South American Indian, straight black hair, skin smooth as porcelain, with a delicate flush of pink. A funnel shaped instrument with baffles slanting to the vent is taken from a leather case and attached to a cutting tube. When the boy sees the funnel he looks at the floor and bites his lips. Two boys carry him to the operating table, one on each side, holding his knees back. They slip the tube in, the funnel protruding. One boy very tall and thin stands in front of the funnel and plays a huge horn of paper-thin copper shaped like a snail shell. There is no sound you can hear, just vibrations shaking the boy inside—now the two sides of his body are rubbing back and forth on the bones until it seems he will split apart and he is spurting up to the chin again and again.

Green boy in a leather jock strap stands there smiling slow and rubbing his jock with one slow finger. A little black boy acts as interpreter. "Him lizard boy. Think plenty slow. No talk much." It takes him three hours in slow motion and when he comes he twists the steel bedstead loose with his hands and bends it into a knot.

Two snake boys with receding foreheads and blue black eyes wearing fish skin jock straps. They have a hissing language sets your teeth on edge. We take them to the cutting room and put tubes up both of them. They lay there looking at each other with unblinking snake eyes. Then one opens his mouth and his fangs spring out an inch long and he bites the other. They are both biting and hissing and shooting yellow jissom all over the sheets. It's the biting brings them off—they quiver from head to foot to get the poison out. We analyzed it later. It's rather like cyanide; kills in a matter of seconds. The snake boys are immune to its effects.

One evening just at twilight I was reading Peter Pan again when I became aware of this *odor* my dear like a rotten sexy corpse and I know it is the Bubu Boys. They are all dressed in pink and purple and yellow shirts to match their sores. They stand there languidly scratching each other and smoking little pipes. The whole thing is mauve and ripe and putrid sweet. We put on rubber gloves and masks. When they strip down in examination no boy undresses himself—another boy does it, then undresses another. They do everything that way—feed each other, light each other's pipes, scratch each other's sores, wipe each other. The sores are a subject in themselves: erogenous, tumescent, suppurating. One boy shows me how he can make a sore crawl all over him and onto another boy. They stand there passing sores back and forth. One points to an eye chart and hits a small *e* across the room with a jet of purple pus. And they can flake sores off to dry dust that will infect for miles downwind.

Well Brad who has a bit of the bad Catholic from a Graham Greene novel screams out: "Greg I have *scruples* about this." I tell him not to be such a silly—is it worse than the Bomb? We must take serum from the sores to use against the *enemy* which can't mind its own business—having no business of its own to mind any more than smallpox does—stringy constipated Spam-eating Christers drop down on decent Indians from a helicopter financed by MRA . . . "Hello Fellows" . . . Well hello your dirty rotten self and give him a water pistol full right in his dead grey teeth. The sores will rot a Wallace folk to the bone in thirty seconds.

When we get one spread his crotch and ass hairs are *erectile.* Tingle hairs they call them—got sex poisons drive you mad to come rotten and Brad lost all control screaming "I don't care if I do go putrid I'll feel the tingle hairs if it's my last act." And I had to kayo him with a joke cutting tube three feet long it isn't funny anymore and Gawd what the sores do when I switch the vibrator on deep massage—they are bursting all over him leaving little craters of erogenous flesh like assholes from head to foot the other boys with their fingers up the sores at the climax he arches his body and hits the ceiling and his skin splits open from crotch to chin. The other boys pull it off in sheets and underneath the boy has a new skin white as marble. They pull the skin off his cock, the one underneath flips out spurting. In this condition after the *moulting* they are so sensitive a breath of air will bring them off.

By the time we are finished they have all moulted off their rotten skins and we leave them to sleep in a dark room. Of course we save the skins and grind them up into a fine powder, like tear gas . . . a bomb or two of dried Bubu skin dropped on New York would make the atom bomb look ridiculous. Think of ten million people going putrid in a matter of seconds—the stink would be a turnon of its own. When they wake up the boys look like Greek statues. They stroll off naked arm in arm through marble porticos and fountains. After a bit they go rotten again and have to moult completely every month. And the skins pile up and up. It's rather like the disposal of atomic waste. We have vats of it and one of many ways to spread it is through birds, which are immune. Just dust it in their feathers and release them to migrate and carry glad tidings to the sunny south.

The Siren Boys are white like a pearl shimmering softly with rippling lights. When we get one spread his ass is a pink mollusc stirring with ecstatic movement reaches out and pulls the cutting tube in. I turn the vibrator on—the boy turns pink then red then deep purple you *ache* to see it—he is vibrating now as the colors flush through him—sky blue salmon pink the Northern lights. Now his lips part and a thin shrill sound comes out that touches nerves and glands inside. The creature comes in a last shrill shriek of ecstacy. Slowly the colors fade back to pearly white. I examine the creature, which lies now in a deep coma, and see that it is a species of mollusc inside a boy shell of soft limestone. They are hermaphroditic beings, able to assume the genitals of either sex. The Siren Boys were developed as a biologic weapon to destroy enemy soldiers and agents. Once they get the siren's touch they are done for. The siren *eats* them slow eating with his whole body. Only the most experienced boys from the Institute of Advanced Sexual Studies are immune to the sirens.

You see we are not just taking cuttings—we are stockpiling sophisticated weaponry. We have all the recordings and the *pictures.* Wallace folk gathered around the TV set to hear the President's State of the Union Message and there in color is a Bubu fucking a Siren, score by the Music Boys. Fat Southern Senator does a triple take, his eyes bug out and explode spraying fluid all over the screen. Indignation was their weapon they were RIGHT RIGHT RIGHT. Well let them choke on it. The Bubus have come to call. Invite you to a church supper and a square dance to follow— round and round faster faster how stands the union? Circus Boy with a hardon squeezing back teeth bare like wild dogs take off your pants and throw them in a corner stay all night and stay a little longer chew your cocaine and spit it on the wall don't see why you don't stay a little longer.

Walter Huston from "The Devil and Daniel Webster" plays the fiddle . . .
Shift partners round and round
Stay all night and stay a little longer
Take off your pants and throw them in a corner
Don't see why you don't stay a little longer . . .
SHIFT PARTNERS ROUND AND ROUND
FASTER FASTER ROUND AND ROUND
Chew your cocaine and spit it on the wall
Grease up your ass and fuck in the hall
Don't see why you don't stay a little longer . . .
FASTER FASTER ROUND AND ROUND
SHIFT PARTNERS ROUND AND ROUND
Golda Meir and Ezra Pound
For Ecology's sake shit on the ground
Don't see why you don't stay a little longer . . .
SHIFT PARTNERS ROUND AND ROUND
FASTER FASTER ROUND AND ROUND
Stay all night and stay a little longer
Take off your name and throw it in a corner
Suck off your buddy and spit it on the wall

Take off your condoms for a VD ball
Don't see why you don't stay a little longer . . .
FASTER FASTER ROUND AND ROUND
SHIFT PARTNERS ROUND AND ROUND
Stay all night and stay a little longer
Take Old Glory and stuff it in a corner
Chew up the Bible and spit it on the wall
The Devil and Webster have come to call
Don't see why you don't stay a little longer . . .

Shift Partners
Round and Round

Top secret classified files . . . Brad reads one and whistles softly looking boyish at the office boy who stares back coldly . . . Then they were called in and asked to resign without prejudice . . .

"Just sign here."

Colonel smokes his pipe with his back to the room . . . two grim grey Army Intelligence men . . . a paper on the desk . . . a pen . . .

It's because some CID bastards had been nosing around in Tangiers where they took their vacations . . .

CID man shows picture to Arab boy who studies it wooden faced. The CID man passes him a note.

"Siiiiii" the boy runs a finger in and out his closed fist . . . "Like beeg one . . ."

"Would you like us to show the infra reds?"

"Why I bought that bastard a drink in The Parade." Greg gasps . . . Boy studies picture. "Si . . . like make party three four boys plenty kief get thrown out Continental Hotel . . . One get caught in sentry box."

"Shall we show the infra reds to the office force?"

"See these men out past the guard sergeant."

Stony faces that had a cheery 'good morning sir' two hours ago. The old sergeant talks without moving his lips.

"I'd try The Advanced Institute . . ."

And here they are in a villa over the sea. This is the clinic, very modern and well equipped. I must explain that at this time our laboratories were working round the clock on the clone project, but we were still dependent on the border cities for male babies, where a semen and baby black market flourished despite periodic crackdowns. You could take your boy friend's semen to town, line up fifty solid Arab girls and take the male crop back to your village.

Here is our agent disguised as a young priest. The cops are pulling semen shakes all over town—you have to keep moving.

Mustapha receives him calmly.

"Sit down my friend and have some tea. First class merchandise sir . . . genuine Bedouin girls."

"Overflow from the Black Cat most likely."

"I have but one word and this I give you . . ."

"Yeah and remember the girl who died of rabies in childbirth and we carted back a horror show werewolf . . . All right bring on the vessels and Doc Monnyham here will look them over."

The doctor is a thin man of fifty, his legs bent with enemy torture and the memory of torture there in his eyes like black pools where fear has died. He looks at the naked girls without expression.

"Friedrick's ataxia, most advanced stage . . . junkie . . . leukemia . . . radiation sickness . . ."

Calm young faces washed in the dawn before creation. The old phallic Gods and the assassins of Alamout still linger like sad pilots in the hills of Morocco to pick up survivors the piper's tune drifts down a St. Louis street with the autumn leaves. The legend of the wild boys grew and all over the world boys ran away to join them. Soon the wild boys were fighting for their lives . . . In the mountains of Northern Mexico a jeep of Operation Intercept. Two Mexican Federales with carbines, two American narcs. A narrow mountain road, sheer drop of black iron cliffs a thousand feet down. The mountainside erupts in a blast—rocks and earth and trees rain down on the screaming fuzz. Now the wild boys appear, looking down, and dust coats their faces frozen into Mayan statues.

Many weapons and boys skilled from childhood in their use. Here is a cyanide injector for use behind enemy lines. It can jet a stream of cyanide like a spitting cobra ten feet. The wild boys have an intelligence network of waiters, bus boys, bellhops, shoe-shine boys . . .

The CIA man hands the shoeshine boy a coin . . .

"Oh thank you sir."

He shoves the injector deep into the man's calf and presses the release . . . As the man slumps forward overturning his whisky the boy walks calmly away . . .

"I think you shit drunk Meester."

Everywhere the wild boys watch and wait . . . LSD in the Colonel's punch, piranha in the swimming pool, black widows in the loo.

Hysterical police machine gun schoolchildren, mistaking a top for a grenade . . . The police by now are a class apart.

Look at these faces that have never seen a woman's face nor heard a woman's voice. Look at the silence. The wild boys will defend their space. They are learning the old magic of wind and rain, the control of snakes and dogs and birds.

Magic of the Juju men who can kill an enemy's reflection in a

gourd of water, weather boys who ride a hurricane across the torn
sky, glider boys on a vast plain surrounded by high black mountains where they live on stone ledges cut in the rock, the roller
skate boys with wings and autogyros soaring across valleys, place
of the dream boys into the deserts of silence and the doors of
empty air, crooning shaman boys the young faces dark with
death, the pure killing purpose blazes from all their faces. Death
to the invaders.

The roller skate boys come to the valley of the glider boys
they whirl the bird men away to a sand dune the boys twist together the bird men making bird calls and the sound of wind on
wings and wires the cry of a hawk the honk of the wild goose birds
and space craft and gliders rise from their bodies over the plain
blue birds and robins perilous gliders over a blue chasm a white
boat under a zeppelin sails across the sky manned by phantom
space cadets from the lost Copenhagen . . . a blue hawk streaks
across the sky fragile spacecraft ships of light skitter like will o'
the wisps, naked boys tend crops and fish ponds in this remote
peaceful area without women splash in stone pools and Frisk has
never seen a woman, Nordic youths swimming in the dead moonlight sad Danish restaurant . . .

"Brad and Greg" he said "Please trust me."

Perhaps somewhere out there done so but I had to know love
and acceptance.

The Colonel looked at me coldly.

"It smells to California."

Here are the boys cooking over campfires quiet valley by a
mountain stream. They have stepped into the dawn before creation. No female was ever made from their flesh that turns to yellow light in the rising sun. The phallic gods of Greece, the assassins of Alamout and the Old Man himself, dispossessed by gener-
ations of female conquest, still linger in the hills of Morocco wait-

ing to pick up the male survivors . . . cool and remote the piper's tune drifts down St. Louis streets with the autumn leaves.

Calling all boys of the earth we will teach you the secrets of magic control of wind and rain. Giver of winds is our name. We will teach you to ride the hurricanes bending palm trees to the ground, high tension wires fall on the police car. We will teach you control of animals birds and reptiles how to pass into their bodies and use them like a knife. We will show you the sex magic that turns flesh to light. We will free you forever from the womb.

South American jungle trail . . . CIA man with a patrol of government troops. He is looking at a map and smoking a cigar.

"What's this area here?"

"Wild boy country señor."

"Are these wild boys political?"

"Not exactly . . . We have a truce with this tribe. It would be a violation of that truce to enter their territory señor."

"Well what are their relations with the guerrilla units?"

"They help sometimes of course since both are outlaws."

"Honor among thieves and cutthroats eh? Help, hide, act as guides do they? Well let's have a look."

Close-up of the CIA man's face . . . his head shrinks to the size of an orange, a little wooden cigar juts from the corner of his mouth . . .

In Morocco here are the bicycle and roller-skate boys who occupy the vast empty suburbs of Casablanca and here is the old skating rink, the roof shattered, afternoon sunlight . . . The boys at a long bench are tinkering with tiny jet engines for their skates, improving crossbows and bolos. One boy is working on a bowie knife with an 18-inch blade. He fits on the ironwood handle with a knob of steel at the end. It is razor sharp, perfectly balanced. The boys have gathered silently around him. The knife passes from hand to hand.

Calm intent young faces in jungle huts, ruined basements, mountain caves, forge and grind and temper the 18-inch blades. This becomes the standard side arm of all the wild boys. Now the maker puts on his jet skates—he starts in the middle of the rink spiraling out faster and faster . . . cantaloupes are set up on posts around the rink. He severs each cantaloupe without moving the two halves, then spirals back to the center and leaps high in the air, swinging the knife in a wild dervish dance, and gives the charge cry.

The wild boys charge down a hillside.

And for every wild boy group there was a like number doing intelligence work and carrying out missions of assassination and sabotage behind enemy lines. The boys rotate intelligence and front line duty. The waiter the bus boy the porter the bellhop the cook—young eyes making the CIA man a ptomaine sandwich.

The roller skate boys ambush a truck of soldiers slinging a 60-foot telephone pole between chains—sweep down a hill and hit the truck broadside, knocking it over, sweep around the truck and cut them to bleeding spurting stumps. I stepped around a gush of blood where a head had been and slipped out a .45 to kill the wounded but the leader a pale metallic Dane said:

"We need the ammunition. Use your knives."

Heads roll, trunks twitch and lay still. We collect the guns.

On screen an old book with gilt edges . . . written in golden script *The Wild Boys* . . . a cold spring wind ruffles the pages . . . pictures fly out . . .

A boy naked except for a blue jock strap sweeps down a mountain road on the edge of precipice, autogyro wings strapped to his shoulders . . . he catapults into space and floats slowly down into the mist of the valley and the sound of running water, distant barking of dogs . . .

Glider boys, wings camouflage, into pink and gold sunset with blue flash laser guns spurting arrows of light . . .

Roller skate boy naked except for his blue steel electronic helmet rocks back holding his knees against his chest. His rectum turns to a pulsing rose of flesh, his body transparent, the delicate limestone tracings of coral along his backbone, the pulsing pearly glands exposed . . . Now the boy is clear blue deeper and deeper blue purple rainbow colors flush through his body as he spurts . . .

Two little desert boys thin as sand foxes fuck on all fours in the light of a campfire. They yelp and bark and their ears tremble as they come against the deep blue sky and the stars like wilted gardenias . . . The roller skate boys dodge down a hill into a hail of bullets that whine off the streets past their ears . . . the 18-inch knives and blue steel helmets glint in the sun . . . lips parted eyes blazing . . .

Beautiful diseased Bubu boys stand by a black lagoon . . .

Dream boys in a 1920 movie, pants down in the vacant lot . . . fragile children of shaded dawn . . .

As I have told you, survivors from the terror of Colonel Driss formed the first wild boy commune. They were holed up in a ruined police barracks with no roof and the boys jacked off in front of their pin-ups every dawn and dusk, like saying prayers. Then one day a boy appeared in the court of the barracks. He was wearing a blue jock strap and he had jet skates with Mercury wings. Surprised in their masturbatory rites the boys turned, cocks in hand, endearments frozen on their lips. He looked at them without any expression at all and jetted away. A high wind sprang up behind him and whipped all the pin-ups from the chipped adobe walls and their clothes from the lines in the court-yard. And we pointed up at the sky where a pair of pants almost caught the NUDEST GIRL IN SWEDEN. We laughed and cheered until we fell exhausted in naked heaps.

From that day to this the wild boys put all thought of women from their minds and bodies. Anyone who joins them must leave women behind. There is no vow. It is a state of mind you must have to make contact with the wild boys. According to the legend an evil old doctor, who called himself God and us dogs, created the first boy in his adolescent image. The boy peopled the garden with male phantoms that rose from his ejaculations. This angered God, who was getting on in years. He decided it endangered his position as CREATOR. So he crept upon the boy and anesthetized him and made Eve from his rib. Henceforth all creation of beings would process through female channels. But some of Adam's phantoms refused to let God near them under any pretext. After millenia these cool remote spirits breathe in the wild boys who will never again submit to the yoke of female flesh. And anyone who joins them must leave woman behind forever.

Two photographers from LIFE spent an uncomfortable flea-bitten fortnight tramping through the Rif and finally posed some street boys on the outskirts of Tangiers, snarling and brandishing knives. This hoax was quickly exposed, like the famous gazelle boy who was allegedly captured after a Jeep had clocked him at 50 miles per hour and who subsequently turned up in Hollywood living with a film producer and starring in Tarzan pictures.

"So far as I am concerned" growled a senior editor, "the wild boys are a myth."

The myth spread and wild boy tribes sprang up everywhere. In the mountains of Northern Mexico, in the swamps of Southern Panama, in the vast Amazon basin and the jungles of Southeast Asia. They have their own language and exchange trade goods over a vast network.

And Brad gave Greg a pair of Mercury sandals for Christmas—jetting along arm in arm, sparks fanning out behind them, they had to laugh at John Citizen his clothes burned full of greasy black holes . . .

Here they are in the Clinic. Boys line up laughing, comparing, jacking off in test tubes. Here is a boy in the cutting room. He is spread out with slings behind his knees and Brad turns a blue light orgone lamp on his rectum and genitals and Greg slips a vibrating cutting tube up him.

His pubic hairs crackle and he blues out and goes transparent—you can see the sperm gathering and pulsing in the pearly glands like an egg tighter tighter the egg explodes shooting gobs of warm light up to the chin . . . A room stacked with embryos in jars with nutrient tubes . . . Brad and Greg move around making adjustments and now fifty boys, some bending over hands on knees, others on all fours or lying down with their legs up . . . Brad throws the switch. The boys writhe and whimper, little phantom figures dance over their bodies, slide up and down their pulsing cocks, get inside their balls and shoot out—

WHEEEEEEEEEEEE

They jet up to the ceiling riding the cutting tube, slide inside their balls squeeze them tighter tighter—the glider boys come robins and bluebirds.

Knees bent, he started down the hill on skates—faster—faster—then he was in the air. He wheeled and banked and turned, those wings were alive now and part of him as he soared in for a landing, touched the pavement, soared again, skipping down the hill like a stone across a lake. Every glider was custom-made to its owner and the wings and fuselage were in many colors, gliding in out of the sunset on red wings like a flight of flamingos, the archers riding the plane with their feet and some use transistor sound effects through electronic helmets—Gnaoua drummers dancing their plane in a steep dive and some German cornballs got themselves up in skeleton suits and came in to funeral marches and mad drag queens formed a Valkyrie Squadron. Next step was a Gemini glider. Just after takeoff a stutter of synapses then they steady down and the wings are talking to each other tossing wind and air currents back and forth and there is a three-man ship controlled by a navigator while his two archers

give all their attention to the target. Wings camouflaged to disappear in a sunset drift down on the west wind and rain poison
arrows from the sky. Wild geese wreck a troop transport plane.
The wild boys are always just out of sight in the colors they cannot see in the places they didn't go . . .

The gliders were camouflaged with painted birds, clouds,
sunsets and landscapes drifting from the sky like autumn leaves,
grey shadows at twilight, cool green ships of grass and streams,
music across the golf course, distant train whistles, lawn sprin-
klers. The old financier nodding on his balcony looked up and saw
a landscape in the sky. It reminded him of an old picture book and
he could see a boy standing there in a stream. As the old man
watched, the boy took a silver arrow from his quiver and raised
his crossbow. A gust of air hit the old man's face and bore his
breath away. Gnaoua dancers dance out of the sky riding their
planes down on the Djemal Fnaa, the black archers leave ten dead
in the square. They have their list and they go through it anywhere in the city . . . the drums of death and the arrows rain
down, no one knows why, no one has seen the list.

The old newspaper magnate who doesn't like to hear the
word *death*, bundled in robes on a deck chair with dark glasses,
was outraged to hear childish voices singing
> "The worms crawl in and the worms crawl out
> They crawl all over your chest and mouth."

He looked up and the sky was full of obituaries piloted by boy
scouts in skeleton masks, each carrying his first single shot .22.
The rifles converged and each rifle had a camera flash popping
away in the sky like firecrackers . . .

An old gentleman was standing by the fireplace. At sight of
me his thin aristocratic face lit up and glowed with incandescent
charm.

"Ahhhh you are the young American . . . How glad I am to

have this assignation with you . . . you must you really must try one of our better brandies . . . in fact rather a great brandy of the house . . . Pierre."

The servant approached discreetly.

"The 69 please."

Something slimy and evil was squirming back and forth between master and servant.

"The 69, monsieur Le Comte?"

"Oui Pierre, le 69."

"Le *vrai* 69, monsieur Le Comte?" he purred out like an obscene old sick tomcat.

"Le vrai 69, Pierre" the count purred back, his eyes narrowed to grey slits. Pierre bowed and retired. The old count seized both my hands in his.

"You must come and stay with us the countess and me in the old château . . ."

"Enchanté charmé oui oui."

"You must you must you must . . ."

"Oui oui oh yes charmed enchanté . . ."

"You must but you absolutely must . . ." He looked deep into my eyes with a quiet intense charm.

"Oh yes oh yes I will will will do it do it really really do it yes I will oh yes oui oui oui . . ."

At this point the jugged hare arrived on my plate, absolutely putrid jet black, inert and repulsive. The old count looked at me across the table, his eyes sharp and quizzical as he sharpened a boning knife with which he would shortly slice paper-thin slices from a seasoned local ham. His beautiful old hands moved deftly under the flickering candles, his voice clear and cold.

"Our recipe for jugged hare dates back to the Crusades and there is an interesting story recorded in our family archives. I am sure our young American guest would like to hear it while he enjoys our modest country hare . . ."

I could feel his sturdy footmen moving closer. Le Comte's

gaze was glassy as he pointed at me playfully with his boning knife.

"Or perhaps our young American friend is so accustomed to buffalo meat that our modest unassuming little hare is beneath his notice????"

Three footmen breathing down my neck, I choked down that putrid paste of a dead animal that stuck to my teeth like rotten tar. What a cover story.

This slimy old Count de Vile has his estate on an island of garbage in an oily lagoon. Our fish boys did the job on him with depth charges. We had learned to breathe under water, we learned very quickly as we learn everything quickly, we are known as 'biologic adaptives'. You run into intolerable currents under these vile oily waters, a proliferating world of film sludge, plots, armies, invisible inaudible screaming for light and sound they fall away like grey shadows. Keep walking. It's not like being under water at all, more like very fine black dust, you have to keep it swirling to let you through. This old Count had been selling diseased lemur Zimbus, many of which died in transit. The future generation of Zimbus is the hope of our party and any attack on a Zimbu is a kick to our crotch.

The Count was receiving an American Bor Bor salesman, one of our undercover men. He knew how anxious the man was to get on with his sale and kept him waiting four hours for dinner . . .

"Would you like to see our portrait gallery? Of course you would . . . How thoughtless of me not to have suggested it before during this rather long lull—you see the servants must always eat first . . . It's a family tradition going back to the Crusades . . . Interesting story connected with it . . ."

Five hours later over brandy and cigars, the Count listened, intent and evil as an old vulture.

"You see it's the perfect drug. You put it in food candy bars soft drinks. It's undetectable and adapts itself to any country. Why it's simply the stupidest sound track of that country. It will bring any area under control. Bor Bor always delivers a majority. Tell me what brand of Bor Bor is sold anywhere and I'll tell you what people think feel hear and see. Now we happen to be looking for an Italian distributor . . . You are the man we want . . ."

Slowly the old Count rose in the air and the walls of his castle crumbled as our depth charge hit.

Day is done

The ill-fated expedition of the Fanatical 80 . . . This was an elite
army of Lesbian commandos known as the Darlings. Each officer
had a bodyguard of policewomen and passive soulful Lesbian or-
derlies and aides-de-camp. Privately financed, they landed on the
coast and penetrated to the heart of wild boy country. But they
never saw a wild boy . . . campfires still warm . . . mocking phallic
drawings on the walls of empty barracks . . .

YOU LIKE BEEG ONE DARLINGS?

The Darlings are in a rubbly hilly area on the outskirts of
Casablanca . . . all around, the howling of dogs. Now they enter a
steep gully.

"COME OUT AND FIGHT YOU FILTHY LITTLE BEASTS!"

Double echo back from the rocky hillside . . .

"COME OUT AND FIGHT YOU FILTHY LITTLE BEASTS . . . Come out and fight you filthy little beasts . . ."

In an old signal tower the wild boys have gathered. They throw back their heads and howl and the howl blurs into a snarl that snaps the head forward, flashing teeth and burning eyes, and all around dogs stir and bristle and run in packs. They break chains and leap over villa walls. They pour out of caves and basements. Now a river of dogs pours into the gully. The Darlings open up with machine guns and grenades but the dogs keep coming, wave after wave, leaping for throat and face, dragging themselves forward on broken hindquarters to hamstring . . . The Darlings are torn to screaming ribbons.

Fifty boys squat in the sand and begin to growl like leopards. Their eyes light up inside, their lips curl back from gleaming fangs . . . now leopards leap down from rocks and trees, a vast horde of leopards streaming forward, the boys trembling snarling flashing forward—it's known as 'riding the cat'. Suddenly the girls see a solid wall of leopards streaking down the canyon wall towards them on both sides. They open up with machine guns but the leopards keep coming leaping over their fallen comrades they tear the Darlings to shreds . . . A leopard growls over a woman's hindquarters, drives another leopard away. Other leopards, satiated, lick the blood from each other's faces.

The boys have ambushed a regiment. Dead soldiers are piled up in a lunar crater. Now the wild boys are outlined on the edge of the crater with their guns against a backdrop of Northern Lights. Audrey points.

"Hey lookit all them dead bodies."

The boys strip off their jock straps and roll around in the dead soldiers like dogs rolling in carrion.

"Got a *liver* knife?" says a slackjawed wild boy.

A boy hands him a little curved knife. He takes the knife and cuts livers out of the youngest and healthiest looking soldiers, checking the eyes for hepatitis. The boys eat the raw liver. They pretend to have TB, coughing and spitting blood all over each other and dying in each other's arms. Finally they all pretend to be dead except for one boy who plays Taps.

Friday, Bellevue 8, 1970 . . . I decided to enunciate the concept of inverse evolution. Man did not rise out of the animal state, he was shoved down to be an animal to be animals to be a body to be bodies by the infamous Fifth Colonists. The animals would have evolved quite painlessly into spiritual phantom lemurs on islands of swamp cypress, antelopes that could run 200 miles an hour, crystal salamanders in deep clear pools, rainbow chameleons and gurkha lizards serenely beautiful, wise old crocodiles with the patience of swamps and rivers in their somnolent eyes, lean delicate frogs, passionate molluscs shimmering with pearly lights in shallow lagoons, great blue crows, the smiling wild dogs . . . In this Eden the first man landed in a crippled spacecraft. He lived there with the animals waiting for a pickup. But the Fifth Colonists arrived. One day when the first man was having intercourse with a shy young lemur he was slapped from behind by a fat cop. The police doctor cut out a rib. The whisky priest muttered over it and it turned into a Lesbian policewoman who screamed at the dazed Adam . . .

"WHAT ARE YOU DOING IN FRONT OF DECENT PEOPLE?"

It started at a garden party given by the Contessa de Vile in Marrakesh. A. J. arrived disguised as a Civil War general, his coat grey and his pants blue.

"Shows how they got together again eh general?"

"Not precisely."

A. J. unsheathed his cavalry saber and with one stroke decapitated the Contessa's Afghan hound. The head bounced across the terrace snarling hideously. In a corner the Electrician tilting the charity pinball machine sent swirls of short circuit through the garden. Glasses and punch bowl crashed to the ground, trays leapt into the air and crashed down on the guests. Mr. Hyslop led in a great grey charger and helped the general into the saddle. The general lifts his bloody sword. Chinese charge in from the kitchen with meat cleavers. The orchestra strikes up The Battle Hymn of the Republic . . .

"He has loosed the fearful lightning of his terrible swift sword . . ."

"LET ME OUT OF HERE!" scream the Aphid Guards. They storm the exits in a whirlwind of severed limbs and bouncing heads.

"He is trampling out the vintage where the grapes of wrath are stored . . ."

In rubber boots and pirate drag with a patch over one eye, the other eye blazing blue, Mr. Hyslop heaves his cutlass up to his knees in blood . . .

"Yo ho ho and a bottle of rum."

He hoists the Jolly Roger as snarling guard dogs hatch from the broken film.

A. J. stands on a pedestal against an evening sky, flags flapping in the wind. He lifts his bugle . . .

"He has sounded forth the trumpet that shall never call retreat . . ."

The sky lights up in a blue flash and slowly darkens as a wild boy plays Taps . . .

"Day is done
Gone the sun
From the lake from the hill from the sky
All is well soldier brave God is nigh . . ."

A. J. stands in a doorway overlooking the courtyard of his palatial Marrakesh residence.

"Where is my cobra God damn it?"

A boy rushes up and thrusts a cobra into his face.

"Here is your cobra meester."

"I don't want the son of a bitch. Put him in the garden."

I walked past him down a hall into blinding sunlight. Too late I realized I had forgotten my spiral pad. The market got darker and darker with a heavy palpable darkness like underexposed film and I blacked out.

I was now dressed in a naval uniform and found myself on the deck of a heaving ship.

"Reef the mizzenmast and hard a starboard you sons of sea dogs," I bellowed out lustily. I signaled to the first mate.

"Detail some men to pour hot tar on the companionway and scrub down the bilge."

I turned on my heel and entered my cabin. Mr. Pike the first mate had followed me in. He sat down insolently in my master's chair and poured himself a tot of rum from a bottle on the table.

"I have to hand it to you sir, to think about spit and polish in a hurricane."

A splintering crash and waves poured through the ruptured hull and swept me out onto the deck.

"Abandon ship God damn it . . . Every man for himself."

The Captain's logbook

A dirigible of India ink moored in a field of wet grass against a violet sky . . . Quivering white pearl boys exploding in opal chips and puffs of white cloud. Pearly labyrinths, fishes of emerald, the yellow light there like honey in my hands . . .

"Dance of rooms dance of faces"—that's from Conrad Aiken, *The Great Circle* . . .

"I've come a long way."

"Cater to seafaring men don't you Mrs. Murphy?"

He took some room with another gentleman. It was a long time ago.

"That room has been closed for years."

"I have the key Mrs. Murphy. You don't remember me Mrs. Murphy? Johnny's back and I can find my way. Ah there you are, stairs behind him . . . fresh in today . . . Here comes Connally's van . . ."

Mrs. Murphy's rooming house . . . all the old showmen . . .

Dry and brittle as dead leaves the scouting party climbed a hill of red sandstone and there was our supply train, half buried in sand . . . thousand miles per hour winds here . . .

Travel, fade out, invisible doors to death and beyond . . .

These youths of image and association now at entrance to the avenue . . .

When Mr. Wilson, the American Consul, arrived at his office he noticed a young man sitting by the reception desk, and hoped that whatever the young man wanted could be handled by the Vice Consul, Mr. Carter.

The man at the reception desk said "Good morning" and passed him the slip. He frowned slightly, glanced at the young man who looked back steadily, and walked up a flight of stairs to his office without reading the slip. It was Monday, the mail stacked on his desk. He spread the slip out.

The phone rang. An inquiry from the English Consulate—

"Yes uh—I don't quite understand what—hmm yess—no not on a tourist visa—" He glanced down at the slip—Name J. Kelly. "No only on a residence visa." Purpose of visit: 'Identity'. What on earth could that mean? Oh God not a lost passport—"You're quite welcome." He hung up.

He flicked a switch. "I will see Mr. Kelly now."

"Yes Mr.—" the Consul glanced down at the slip though of course he had memorized the name—"Mr. uh Kelly—and what can I do for you?"

The young man sitting across the desk had a suntanned face and very pale grey eyes. 'A merchant seaman' the Consul decided, removing from his face any trace of warmth, 'lost his money and passport in a whorehouse,'

"I understand it was you who wanted to see me."

"I—" The Consul was disconcerted. He remembered something about a passport left as security for a bill—Kelly was it? He looked for the slip in a letter basket, ah here it was—passport No. 32, USA, left as security, Hotel Madrid . . .

The Consul was very severe now. "May I see your passport please."

To his surprise the young man immediately handed over a passport which he had apparently held concealed behind the desk. The Consul examined the passport.

It was a seaman's passport, No. 18—'Hmm these low numbers—date of birth 1944, San Francisco—' The Consul looked up.

"There has been a mistake here. It was a different Kelly I wanted to see."

The young man nodded. "I know that. My brother."

"You knew about it did you? Then why did you come instead of your brother?"

"My brother Joe Kelly is dead."

"Dead? But when? Why hasn't the Consulate been informed?"

"He died five years ago."

The Consul prided himself on his imperturbability. He studied the slip, recalling it had come to his desk just as he was leaving the office on Friday afternoon—

"Well Mr. Kelly, obviously there is some mistake all round. After all it is not an uncommon name. What makes you think this notice refers to your brother in any case?"

"Is the notice dated?"

"Dated? Why it came to the office Friday afternoon."

"Yes but does it have a date on it?"

The Consul looked at the slip. The date was smudged, illegible. In fact, the Consul had to concede there was something odd about the notice. It seemed to be a photostatic copy, like some old document from a forgotten attic, stating simply that the Hotel Madrid was holding Passport 32 issued in the name of one Joe Kelly, born February 6th, 1944, San Francisco, California—for/ against nonpayment of Hotel Bill (amount not specified), signed by the manager J. P. Borjurluy.

The Consul pursed his lips and picked up the phone. "I have a notice here"— he read the notice over the phone. "When did that come in? Friday—at what time?—and who brought it? Hmm." He hung up.

"Well this is odd. Seems the man at the desk had stepped out for a moment and found the notice on his desk when he returned ... Mr. Kelly, could you tell me the circumstances of your brother's death?"

"S.S. Panama out of Casablanca for Copenhagen—went down with all hands."

It so happened that the Consul was a collector of sea disasters, on which he kept a scrapbook of clippings. The Mary Celeste, The Great Easter, The Morro Castle. Here was one he had missed—minor perhaps, small freighter, however in view of—he glanced at the slip—decidedly worth looking into.

He took out a package of Players, smiling for the first time, and offered the open package to his visitor. The young man accepted the cigarette with a deadpan "Thanks."

There was, the Consul decided, something, well *remarkable* about the pale cold eyes that seemed to be looking at some distant point far away and long ago. 'He is looking through a telescope' the Consul decided, with a certainty that surprised him.

"I gather your brother was a member of the crew?"

"Yes. He was the third mate."

"Any passengers aboard?"

"One. A young Dane called Leif. Ran out of money—'blank', the Danes call it—he was as the Danes say 'blank'. Repatriated by his Consul."

"Not quite."

"Not quite? No not quite—about fifty sea miles short."

The Consul reminded himself that Monday was a busy day.

"Well I suggest we go along to the Hotel Madrid this after-noon." He leafed through his appointment book. "Could you meet me here at 4 p.m.?"

It is a clear sparkling autumn day. You can see the towers on the Rock with the unaided eye. The telescope is now pointed at the towers. Seen through the telescope, the towers shimmer as if in a heat haze. I take a picture of the telescope and the swimming pool, avoiding palm trees. Yes the garden could be

Sweet Meadows 1,
Nov. 4, 1970

The selective visitors to Puerto de los Santos of the Farout Is-lands, while waiting to locate themselves in permanent quarters, usually stay at Hampton House. This is a barracks-like wooden structure high in the town, which is built on a series of terraces and cliffs from a thousand feet down to sea level. The food at Hampton House is good and what a tenant does in his room is his affair. Walking in the streets I was struck by the deep blue of the sea, the flowering trees and shrubs everywhere. The inhabitants wore bright colors and wide smiles but there was something sleazy about them, I thought. The temperature here is about 80 degrees, and I noticed people walking about naked. It looked like a nice place on the whole, but I heard apartments were difficult and many had grown old in Hampton House waiting for one—and here was Ian who had something absolutely fabulous the day after his arrival.

He was showing me around. Quite near the sea, built of natural stone, balconies all around, Persian rugs, the lot.

"However did you do it?"

"Oh," he told me "it has been arranged through the Consul . . ."

I had met the Consul at the airport and received a very bad impression. A seedy pock-faced man in a dirty grey linen suit, he jerked a thumb at his chest.

"Me your Consul Meester. You need something you come to me. Plenty bastards here."

He gave me his dirty card: "Filipe Cardenas Infanta, Honorary American Consul". And now Ian was talking of giving him six hundred dollars on some vague assignment of a lease he probably had no right to negotiate—Ian, who was always so careful about such things. Perhaps the climate was enervating and one couldn't quite ignore the fact that as we sat on the balcony with the scent of flowering trees, looking across the harbor, the natives were everywhere—walking by the balcony on a causeway, perched in trees, clambering over the roof. Still, the climate is superb.

At the highest point on the island, about three thousand feet, a great gorge stretches down to the sea. At the pinnacle of the gorge a limestone cliff drops away a thousand feet straight down . . .

Every Sunday the levitation students launch themselves from this platform of natural stone, sail down and land on the beach, waving to their companions in the air. Naked, in bathing suits, rainbow jock straps, Buck Rogers outfits and Mercury sandals—it's a dazzling sight, and sometimes an *espontáneo* from the onlookers will try his wings. Some of them fly. It's all in the perfect confidence you understand . . . and here is Ian's house, quite near the sea; Persian carpets the lot, flowering trees and shrubs, bright colors, wide smiles . . . absolutely fab sea level food at Hampton's he was showing me around in his room is his affair stone balconies all round blue rock by the sea . . . However did you do it? Couldn't quite ignore a seedy pock-faced man . . . "Me your Consul meester . . . You need roof."

Soldier brave

Outskirts of Singapore . . . Rickshaw pulls up in front of a shabby bar: NUMBER I BAR. A young man gets out. He is yellow-haired and wearing a yellow pongee silk suit. His face is lined and drawn, older than his years, the eyes wary and pinned out with morphine. He needs a shave and his suit is dirty. He pays off the boy and walks in.

There is one table of customers in the bar. They all turn and look at him. He walks over to the bar, where the bartender is also looking at him, silent and impassive.

"Do I have the right address? Cantina de Los Santos?"

"Name change." the bartender says.

A grey-haired red-faced man gets up from a table.

"You have the right address, friend, and welcome to the

lodge. This is Rodriguez the bus driver." Flashback shows burning bus sequence.

"And this is Jimmy the pilot." Flashback shows pilot bailing out of passenger plane.

"And this is Doc Lee . . . He's a bit shorthanded on a construction job and not too particular about his personnel . . . Right, Doc?"

That's right—few things in my own past I'd just as soon forget . . ."

"And I—" says the young man . . . "I was the third mate on the Titanic. Got in the first lifeboat in women's clothes. Spot of bother when the women recognized me but with God's help and a submachine gun I sorted it out . . ."

God is nigh

"I had secured a position upriver in Malaya, supervising a crew of one hundred coolies who would under my direction allegedly construct a railroad . . . as it happens, the railroad was never completed . . ."

Voice of the narrator as he is seen unpacking in bungalow with a slender Malay houseboy. James Lee is unpacking his drug case, which is a large doctor's satchel, placing bottle and pipes and syringes on the table while Ali unpacks suits and mosquito netting and rifles and tinned food.

"I was by now established on a wholesome regime of four morphine injections per day mixed with cocaine, six pipes of opium before retiring, and hashish throughout the day to keep up my appetite and enhance sexual vigor. The same regime was of course followed by Ali my houseboy . . ." Lee and the houseboy strip and make it after a series of judicious injections.

"The coolies were housed in one Bongsal, a huge room like a circus tent with beds, tents, cubicles, mats, and cooking stands. Since there were no women within a hundred miles, it is not surprising that other vices abounded . . ." James Lee is seen inspecting the Bongsal in a haze of hashish and opium smoke.

"I found that the young boys were enslaved by a clique of tattooed gangsters from Singapore who sold them and gambled them back and forth. I determined to end this evil practice." Scenes of gambling the boys, etc.

"Accordingly, when a traveling executioner arrived at the village I paid him a large fee, and brought cases against the ringleaders, who were beheaded on the spot . . ." The boys rush forward and bathe in the blood.

"Freed from coercion, the boys became the masters and nightly orgies were carried out in the Bongsal. After the day's work and a bath in the river, the coolies would gather in the Bongsal to cook, wash clothes, smoke opium and hashish. Soon the boys were stripping off their clothes . . ." A boy dances stark naked to drums and flutes.

"When I entered with Ali, the scene was indescribable . . ." James Lee enters the Bongsal with his satchel.

"As I threaded through the naked men and boys, friendly hands divested me of every garment, but I refused to surrender my drug case and I was soon putting it to good use. I observed two young boys copulating but experiencing difficulty in reaching a climax, owing to overindulgence in opium. Already the onlookers were shuffling their feet and looking away as the remedy sprang to hand. Deftly I injected half a grain of cocaine into one boy's buttocks and that portion of the other boy's buttocks which I could conveniently reach . . ." The boys spring to life. The onlookers are riveted. The boy comes all over James Lee, who sits down naked on a cane seat and opens his drug case.

"I now passed out a candy made from Yage which I had brought back from Brazil and hashish with certain irritants that set up an itchy red erogenous rash in the genitals and anus as sexual visions careened through the brain cooled by the cool blue calm of the Yage. Soon the boys were prowling about like animals, coupling here and there, surrounded by masturbating onlookers. The huge room was suffused with the smell of rectal mucus, sperm, sweat, hashish and opium. I myself was soon involved and fucked on all fours by a red-haired Malay boy who undoubtedly carried some sailor's blood in his veins. I could feel the young sailor's face smiling into mine as I came in front of my hundred coolies in pure fearless blue flame of Yage spiced with hashish and further cooled and tempered by opium, then unleashed by cocaine.

"I established myself as a Holy Man and peace reigned in the Bongsal. When fights occasionally broke out, I promptly administered morphine to both participants. We had by now set up refining plants to make both cocaine and morphine. Ali and I moved the bed and furniture into the Bongsal and set up a little corner of England with my family pictures and school banner. The Bongsal was like a small town under one roof with cubicles, cooking stalls, tier of bunks, hammocks, pet parrots, monkeys and jackals.

"I took care to establish a schedule of rotation. There were cool blue Yage nights with flute music and delicate remote copulations. There were wild pounding hashish and cocaine nights that crackled through the Bongsal as fuck lines formed to wild music. And there were calm sane nights on number two—opium—when everybody did what he wanted to do.

"As you see my system is based on rotation of the drugs used, and the same principle applies to any activity. Those who have experienced the heights of sexual pleasure will endeavour to do so again at the first opportunity and thereby will soon exhaust themselves and dull the sensation they covet. So after a strenuous orgy, on the following night I would give each man a large injection of morphine and continue these injections for several nights, tempering them gradually with cocaine to prevent constipation and lethargy, and then with hashish until the men were again in condition.

"We managed to drag the railroad out for five years, and happy years they were."

From early childhood Jerry has been a physical coward. He simply cannot stand any pain. He is doubly vulnerable by his addiction to any pleasure. He loves sweets and ice cream and good food, and to have a meal delayed even for fifteen minutes causes him the most acute salivating discomfort and loud petulant stomach rumbles. In adolescence his erections are uncontrolled and often embarrassing. This embarrassment can pass to the exquisite pleasure of spontaneous orgasm.

This occurs for the first time with the director of the Academy he is attending. The director has just been to the Clayton house for dinner. Jerry's mother and father are out. He is sitting in the living room with the director, feeling very ill at ease as he tries to make conversation. The director is looking at him silently and suddenly says:

"I'd like to see you stripped Jerry."

Jerry feels suddenly weak. Suppose it happens? He *knows* it will happen.

"Oh all right . . . Up in my room?"

He walks ahead of the director up the stairs. He is breathing heavily and his heart pounds. In his room a .22 rifle on the wall, some sea shells in a glass case, rose wallpaper. The director is asking him about his schoolwork as he takes off his tie and jacket. He is getting his mind off it, maybe it will be all right. He keeps talking as he unbuttons his shirt and takes it off. He drops his shoes rather loudly on the floor. He stands up and the director looks at him.

"Come over here Jerry."

Awkwardly Jerry walks over and stands in front of him. The man undoes his belt unbuttons his pants and shorts and they fall to his ankles he can feel the weight in his crotch as he steps out of his pants and shorts and stands there with nothing on but his short sox. The man puts his hands on Jerry's back and chest . . .

"Stand up straight . . . That's right . . ."

The director is looking down at his body and it is happening he can't stop it . . . He blushes bright red and bites his lip with a little whimpering sound.

"Your little pecker is getting hard . . ."

As Jerry knows it is all right his embarrassment turns to excitement as the man turns him around, touching him here and there and correcting his posture.

"Sit down Jerry . . ."

Jerry sits down on the bed beside him.

"Have you been playing with your pecker Jerry?"

Jerry blushes. "Well uh I touch it sometimes . . ." Actually he has never jacked off awake, though he has wet dreams several times a week.

"Have you ever played with it until it went off?"

A drop of lubricant squeezes out the slit of Jerry's cock . . . "Went off? You mean that?" He points to the pearl of lubricant.

"No Jerry not that. It's something that happens when you play with it . . ."

With caressing fingers he touches the crown of Jerry's cock.

"Are you circumcised Jerry?"

He runs his fingers down to see if the the penis is circumcised or protruding from a loose foreskin . . . As his fingers touch Jerry feels the wet dream in his tight nuts gasping head back he goes off.

Jerry is a strange creature like a stranded mollusc. He blushes easily and when frightened he turns a pale green. Once while riding in the back seat of his father's Dodge he went off in his pants in a road dip. After that he always got a hardon riding in cars and this was frequently embarrassing. Here he is getting out of a car trying to hide it with a hand thrust forward in his pocket.

As soon as his father and older brother drove away in the car, Jerry hurried up the back stairs through his father's studio into his own room and pulled the package he had received in the post that morning from under the bed, opening it with trembling fingers. It was a vibrator with a blunted red rubber rod attached. Mouth dry heart pounding he kicked off his moccasins and peeled off his shirt and shoved down his pants and shorts. His cock hard and lubricating he took a jar of vaseline from a drawer and lay down on the bed with his legs up and rubbed the vaseline on the end of his vibrator and up his ass which opened now and seemed to suck the vibrator in. He sighed deeply and pressed the switch kicking his legs in the air feeling the wet dream tension in his crotch and just as he was coming he saw his father and brother standing over the bed. Jerry blushed bright red to his bare feet still holding the vibrator in he couldn't stop and went off spurting up to the chin choking gasping in a red haze his legs kicking spasmodically silver spots boiled in front of his eyes and he blacked out.

When he came to, his father was rubbing his face with a cold towel and his brother was smiling and unbuttoning his shirt.

This sexual rapport with his father and brother was a great release for Jerry. He took lessons in Jiu Jitsu and began to get over his physical cowardice. But storm clouds were gathering. His father had never been a good businessman.

"By and by hard times came a-knocking at the door."

They lost the big house on the hill and moved into a small apartment with thin walls and hostile neighbors. His brother was killed in a car accident. A year later his father and mother died in an epidemic of scarlet fever. He was sent to live with an uncle who was going to make a man out of him by sending him to a military school. So Jerry ran away to join a traveling circus.

Oh oh
what can the matter be?

It was bitterly cold on the Halifax wharf, clear and bright in late sunshine. The fresh offshore wind had dropped somewhat when John Hamlin reached the Mary Celeste. He had signed on as third mate. As he stepped aboard he saw a boy standing about ten feet in front of the gangplank, as if to welcome him aboard. The boy was about sixteen, with a pale wasted face, green eyes and ruffled brown hair. There was a jagged half-healed scar on the left cheek-bone, livid in the red rays of the setting sun. Dressed in a blue shirt and tattered grey jacket, he seemed not to notice the cold. As he looked at John his lips parted in surprise and recognition. His eyes lit up inside and he smiled like an animal licking his lips, virginal lust naked in the young face. A gull dropped a scrap of bread at the boy's feet. He stepped closer like a wary street cat,

plaintive and tentative. A sweet sour rotten musky smell drifted
from his half-open mouth. John wondered if the boy was normal.
He smiled and held out his hand.

"I'm John, the third mate."

The hand in his was smooth and thin and cold.

"I'm Audrey your cabin boy only I'm too sick to work really
or sleep in the forecastle you understand of course so we'll be
sharing a cabin that is if you want me for your cabin boy . . ."

He trailed off weakly and began to cough, turned aside into
the setting sun and covered his face with a blue bandanna, his
whole body shaking. John put a hand on the boy's shoulder, feeling the bones like a starved cat's. Finally the boy stopped coughing and put the bandanna into his coat pocket. He looked at John,
his lips flecked with blood, smiling as he licked the blood in with
the last red rays of the setting sun his face blazed like a comet and
dimmed out as the sun sank behind a cloud over Halifax.

(Cut in shot of the Halifax Explosion 1910.)

The shadow of night fell on the boy's face, on the rigging and
the circling gulls. John felt the chill of empty space. The boy's face
was covered with a white crust of frost, and splinters of ice glittered in his ruffled hair eerie and ghostly in the twilight . . .

"I hope my coughing doesn't keep you awake . . ."

He led the way to a door and into a cabin. Kerosene light
picked out two bunks, lockers, a wash stand with mirror, a bowl
of water hyacinths in a bracket. The hyacinths filled the small
cabin with a sweet flower smell in which floated the musky sour
smell of the boy's breath.

"Mind if I smoke sir?"

Without waiting for an answer the boy rolled a cigarette and
lit it. His smile through cigarette smoke was the smile of an insolent street boy looking for scraps of advantage.

"If you'll pardon me sir the crew is terrible folk. There'll be
trouble on this trip sir. And I want you to know you can count on
me . . . as a *friend* sir."

"I'm sure I can, Audrey. And let's keep it that way, shall we?"

"I can tell you everything goes on in the forecastle sir . . . though it's very dangerous for me to talk to you like this . . ."

"Perhaps you'd better shut up then."

Audrey polished his nails on his coat lapel and looked at them. "Would you care for some opium sir? It helps to keep your mind off women sir."

John ignored this and began unpacking his sea bag. "It smells like a florist shop in here. Who put these flowers in the cabin?"

"Oh that would be Jerry sir." Audrey went on looking at his nails. "He's a right fag. I hate them sir don't you?"

"No."

"I know what you mean sir . . . I've thought about it too . . ." Audrey licked his lips and rubbed his crotch.

"Shut up. Shut up and get me a cup of coffee."

The boy's face seemed to break up and suddenly he burst into tears. "Don't you understand who I am?"

A chill settled over John's recognition . . . "Audrey the ice boy."

Frost on his face splinters of ice glittered in his hair virginal lust naked in the last red light a scrap of bread at the boy's feet. The boy dimmed out in the rigging and circling gulls . . .

"I'm Audrey your chill of interstellar space John."

Your cabin there his ruffled hair in the cabin wasted face left cheek bone . . . broken bottle . . .

"Hey lookit all them dead bodies . . ."

Seemed not to notice the cold as Audrey points with his left hand. His eyes lit up inside like a topping forest fire. Smiled like an animal virginal from remote seas of past time plaintive sad survival. A musky smell of open years drifted from his open years waiting for this.

"I'm John."

Wind across the boy's face pale on the wharf. He coughed into his handkerchief. "It's TB sir . . . Took two of my brothers . . . Let me tell you about the crew sir . . . There's Johnny Cyanide did a cyanide swallowing act in carny . . . Fire eating too . . ."

Carnival flashback . . . "Hey Rube."

Johnny takes a swig of gasoline and spits fire at the advancing crowd, singeing hair and setting clothes on fire . . . burning circus tent . . .

"He can crush a raw potato with his grip or stick his finger through it . . . And he does a hanging act with young Jerry that's a thing to see sir . . ." Audrey rubbed his crotch and twisted his head to the left and made a clicking sound with his tongue. John looked at him coldly and he went on quickly.

"And there's Pecos Bridge Juanito the knife thrower . . ."

Juanito sitting naked in a chair throws a knife and cuts a scorpion in two on the wall . . . Moonlight on a dusty street little Texas town. Whispering Tom Mayfield with twenty greaser notches in his gun steps from a doorway . . .

"All right you fucking Mexican stop right there."

Juanito clasps his hands behind his head and pivots slowly at first then suddenly speeds up throwing a knife from a holster behind his neck. It catches the sheriff in the Adam's apple and he flops like a stricken buzzard.

"And Jerry his assistant, who throws knives with his toes . . ."

Jerry Tyler, a slim red-haired boy about Audrey's age, naked on his back with his knees up. He is lying on a padded platform. He grasps two handholds and takes a knife from a rack with the toes of his right foot. He flexes his leg. His lips draw back, showing his teeth. His cock stiffens and stands up straight from his stomach as he straightens his leg. The knife thuds into a side of beef as the boy ejaculates.

"And there's Davy Jones . . . No one can figure him sir . . ."

St. Louis courtroom. Davy Jones is called. He stands in front of the judge, insolent and poised.

"The Chinese cook and his assistant the Frisco Kid . . ."

Ghostly scene in the galley. The Chinese cook, unhurried and old and nothing caring. The Frisco Kid pale and remote . . .

"And there's a Filipino boy who never talks . . . He's got a dreamy look in his eyes sir . . ." Shops' shutters slamming in an Eastern market . . .

"AMOK AMOK AMOK . . ."

"And *Francis* Jones he calls himself . . . The sweetest voice you ever heard sir . . . And look what I found in his sea bag sir . . ." Audrey holds holds out a police wanted-poster:

"Frank alias Francis alias Christopher Jones" . . . picture of a youngish man with a waxed mustache and a smooth plump face . . . "Wanted for bank robbery and murder . . ."

1918 bank . . . Jones and three others walk in. A sweet voice echoes through the bank . . .

"Everybody please put your hands up high."

A teller reaches for a gun. Jones shoots him twice through the chest and he slumps spitting blood, as a terrible gloating expression surfaces in Jones's smooth waxen face.

"And three Swede brothers who look around the forecastle and sneer sir . . ."

The three Swedes wreck a bar like a tornado.

"And don't forget the cargo sir . . . *alcohol* sir . . . How wouldn't those Swedes like to dip into that? . . . Have you met the skipper yet?"

"Yes."

Flashback shows the skipper, who has a thin Germanic face and green eyes as he passes John the pen to sign on with. He speaks with a slightly ironic inflection as he glances down at the signature.

"You have made a wise decision uh John."

"He's known as Opium Jones in the trade sir . . . opium, white slaving, nothing is too dirty for Opium Jones . . . And he's a right savage buzzard as well . . . Telling you all this could cost me my life sir . . . Why only this morning one of those Swedes grabbed me by the collar sick as I am sir and slapped me across the face sir and said . . . 'You one little stool pigeon bastard' . . . I'd appreciate something for my defense sir . . . If you could get me a revolver from the armory . . ."

"Certainly not. And I'll make up my own mind about the crew."

Audrey polished his nails and looked at them . . . "Perhaps it will be the other way around sir . . ."

Flash forward of ship under sail. One of the Swedes looks after John and spits on the deck.

"Another fairy on this Hell ship."

John meets the first mate, who carries a sawed-off shotgun. He smiles, and his eyes glint cold as ice in sunlight.

"If there's one thing I'm sure of, John, it's that you and I are *friends*."

Johnny's so long
at the fair

Carnival flashbacks . . . Johnny Cyanide who also spits fire and swallows swords, and he can make a sword pop out his mouth and stick into a target. He can break a two-by-four with the side of his hand, tear two decks of cards in two, and crush a raw potato with his grip or stick a finger through it. Juanito the knife thrower, who can throw a knife and cut a moving cockroach in two, and Jerry Tyler his assistant, who throws knives with his toes.

An albino morphine addict called Andy the Hanged does a hanging act with a gimmicked rope all in pink sequins. The morphine has turned his face a grey green color like an underground mushroom. To see him hanging there kicking with his pink eyes rolled back in his head is an unwholesome sight and it packs in the marks. In St. Louis he ran out of junk, forgot to check his rope and went on sick, broke his neck and went off in his pink sequins with the spotlight on him and that was a powerful sight. Johnny got him down but he died during the night. So Johnny takes over the act. Then he gets Jerry in as his assistant to play a young cowhand caught with a running iron.

Johnny Cyanide and Jerry on the gallows. Suddenly a crowd of drunken cowhands and miners surges in.

"GET OFF THE GALLOWS YOU FUCKING FAGS OR WE'LL HANG YOU FOR REAL."

"HEY RUBE!"

Jerry unlocks his manacled hands with a key in his teeth, drops behind the gallows and pulls a bolt, and a pride of tigers leaps out.

Any place but there

St. Louis flashbacks . . . One day in Masserang's Drug Store Mrs. Greenfield bought me a chocolate soda and I saw her in action. An eager Jew woman gushed up to the table.

"Oh Mrs. Greenfield . . . So nice to see you . . ."

Mrs. Greenfield inclined her head and flashed her icy smile. The Jew woman is on about this party she's been to and Mrs. Greenfield says . . . "You were very fortunate weren't you?" holding her there squirming like a big brown carp begging for mercy that did not come.

And Mrs. Greenfield's husband the Colonel was one of the bores of all time. He'd spent the first World War in Paris as a young lieutenant, and he liked to ramble on about that period in his life. "This woman so beautiful she was a Goddess actually and

I once spent the night sleeping in front of her door. I think any real Southern gentleman will understand."

Another one he laid on me was how he was coming home from a late party when this little French fairy approached him . . . "It was a cold night and the rain was streaming down and he didn't have an overcoat and no shoes. So I led him to believe his proposition was acceptable to me and when we reached the door of my lodgings I knocked him into the gutter where he belonged and slammed the door."

"Well" I said, "Wasn't that a bit much . . . After all, customs of the country, you know."

"If any son of mine went queer I'd kill him with my own hands. And if I thought the son of any friend of mine was a queer I'd kill him too . . ."

Now I belonged to a boy scout troop, and we'd been taught Karate to defend ourselves against child molesters so without more ado I slammed a knee into his crotch and stabbed a spear hand deep into his purple throat. He hit the floor and I finished him off with my scout knife. Three times I dragged his body around the block behind my Red Bug.

"He molested me" I told the fuzz with a boyish sob. And I was awarded the Red Cross for bravery.

Prep School flashbacks . . . Cab stopped just ahead under a streetlight and a boy got out with a suitcase, thin kid in prep school clothes . . . familiar face the Priest told himself reminds me of something a long time ago the boy there reaching into his pants pocket for the cab fare . . .

Dim dead boy so I haunted your old flower smell of young nights on musty curtains empty prep school clothes further and further away. Come closer. Listen across backyards and ash pits. Sad old human papers I carry. I was waiting there . . .

Asshole sunrise St. Louis morning outside stands over me naked one foot in a sweat sock rubbing my cock.

"I want to cornhole you Billy."

Sighed and squirmed spread my legs sweat quivering what that means down on the bed on my stomach.

The boys stand in front of the bureau. Audrey is a thin pale blond boy with a large pimple where his buttocks crease. John is red-haired with green eyes.

"Show you something Audrey."

He opens a drawer and there is the vibrator with a blunted red rubber rod. Audrey knew at once what it was for. His mouth went dry and his heart pounded and silver spots boiled in front of his eyes. He walks to the bed and lies down on his back holding his knees against his stomach. Now John kneels between his legs. He greases the vibrator and slowly shoves it in.

"Here you go Audrey."

He presses the switch. Audrey felt a soft pink mollusc squirm through his body and saw himself suddenly transparent prostate pulsing a great pearl in ecstasies of exposure the quivering pimple whiffs of his feet in the warm 1920 afternoon as colors flush through his body ... reds that dissolve him to jelly he was skinned there choking in a red haze intestinal mauves and browns and sepias steam off his body silver light pops in his eyes and he is spurting out of his body in soft warm globs.

Subject taught in the school: Seeing with the whole body.

Jerry leans over and grabs his ankles and grins between his legs. The boys circle him, each boy stopping to look. Now the Mexican kid is looking at him and it happens. Jerry is seeing him with his ass and the backs of his thighs. He shivers and turns bright red all over, goose pimples spatter his body, his ass crinkles and the Mexican kid is seeing him with his stiffening cock and his thighs and stomach. Kiki moves forward and slides it in. The two bodies quiver together as if in contact with a high tension wire vibrating from head to foot as a heavy purple smell of ozone reeks out of them. The smell acts on the boys like catnip. They roll around their legs in the air kicking fucking rimming giggling out hot spurts made machine gun noises as he came.

Subject taught in the school: The use of sex rays.

In the orgone room lined with magnetized iron the boys peel off their Rasurel underwear in showers of blue sparks. Slowly silently the musky flower smell of young hardons fills the room. There is a sweet metal taste in Audrey's mouth that spreads and tingles through him as he bends over and holds his ankles spreading his ass little blue eyed twilight grins between his legs. A boy picks up a small accumulator like a ray gun and points it at Audrey's ass. It hits like soft pebbles of light crinkling and vibrating his ass. Another boy stands in front of him and trains the ray on his crotch. His balls crinkle and tighten soft blue sparks crackle in his pubic hairs. Another boy throws himself down on a bed spreading his legs and holding his feet in the air as the ray hits his ass and balls and cock his body contracts in a fluid spasm throwing sperm up to his chin. Audrey's whole body vibrates out of focus the hairs stand up on his head and he grins his back teeth bare like a wild dog. The musky blue ozone smell reeks out of him as he comes the Milky Way . . .

The boys stand in a blue twilight and repeat the school oath:

"A Wild Boy is filthy, treacherous, dreamy, vicious and lustful."

Patrol comes to police post . . . sentry dead . . . cyanide dart . . . inside three soldiers, throat cut to the backbone . . . gun racks empty . . . Take a look at this gadget . . . Into a leather strap razor blades have been sewn, loaded at one end with a lead weight, a wood handle at the other end . . . whipped around the neck from behind and here is a strangling cord with a ratchet like those suitcases you stack with clothes and then sit on once tightened it can only be released by pressing the catch.

In the swampy coastal cities Siren Boy-Girls who can assume the form of either sex lure the soldiers to ecstatic death, rotting their bodies with erogenous sores . . .

Boys on high towers raise their arms . . . WIND WIND
The wind rises and the boys are in the sky now, riding the hurricane, throwing water against the sea wall, feeling the trees give and break, houses thrown around like matchsticks, rivers bursting their banks . . .
WIND WIND WIND
The twisting black fury of a tornado darkening his young brow spinning around him pulling down motels and supermarkets tossing trucks on their sides . . .
WIND WIND WIND
Streaking across the dark sky . . .

Flying bicycles, gliders launched from skates and skis, strange sky crafts with sails stabilized by autogyros . . . a blue hawk shoots out of the boy's head across the sky, from their bodies flights of robins and bluebirds, herons and wild geese . . .

And here are the dream boys who dream awake, and their dreams can be seen like phantoms in the still air, and the silent boys who never speak and live where words are impossible. Few can breathe there.

A patrol of wild boys has camped on the edge of the Blue Desert, home of the little desert boys, shy and skittish as sand foxes with flaring ears, eyes glinting as they prowl hungrily around the camp. A boy holds out a piece of meat and one of the desert boys comes forward. The boy takes his wrist and pulls him into his lap. The desert boy struggles for a few seconds then lies still gasping as they strip off his loincloth and hold his legs back masturbating him and running a finger over his rectum he trembles yelps ejaculates . . .

Other desert boys come into the camp now two of them fucking on all fours, ears trembling, braces himself looking at the sand and they show their sharp little teeth in squeals and yelps and barks. Now the desert boys cuddle against their bodies under blankets whimpering in sleep . . . dream copulation in the deserted quarry, semen spurting over limestone streaked with rust . . .

A room in Mexico, outside blue sky and wheeling vultures over a great empty valley. Inside plaster walls painted dark blue. Two boys sitting on a brass bed. In the middle of the room is a rocking chair of yellow oak with a leather cushion. The boys are looking at the rocking chair, which oscillates slightly in the afternoon wind. As they look they lick their lips and get hardons. Kiki walks over and sits down. He motions to Audrey, a thin pale boy with yellow hair. Audrey straddles Kiki's legs facing him and slowly squirms down onto Kiki's cock. The boys begin to rock back and forth phallic shadows on the blue wall faster and faster with a pumping motion. Suddenly their feet brace and they quiver together silent intent faces calmed to razor sharpness and blue sparks flash from their eyes.

Another room with yellow wallpaper. Kiki pulls Audrey

down onto his lap. They rock back and forth showing Kiki's tight brown nuts below Audrey's nuts crinkled in yellow hair pink curtains moving slightly in the afternoon breeze the boys are running together asses and cocks and tight balls dissolving in hula hoops of light that move up and down their bodies the room vibrates and shakes the walls crack and the boys ride the rocker across the sky.

Somewhere a long time ago the summer ended. Old pulp magazines on the white steps. Grimy pants stood clearly even the stains. Last time together last dust of hope out there in the blue flight of adolescence on road of the Stranger. Remember who the Stranger was breathing the writer's self-knowledge and God guilt? Remember who the Stranger was breathing leaves in red hair your smell of peanuts in his hand? An obscene word scrawled on the further shore long ago. Cold dust of the dead boy a last trip home across the gleaming empty sky fragments of lost words will you his last expedition. Long long how long in the lost town heard he was a caddy years later.

From the lake
From the hill

Harbor Beach is a little postcard town on Lake Huron. The town slopes up from the lake onto low hills, neat white frame houses, steep winding streets. The hills are very green in summer, surrounded by meadows and fields and streams with stone bridges, and further inland woods of oak and pine and birch. The summer people have cottages there and a whole town to themselves, where most of them eat in a communal dining hall to which they are summoned by a bell, and ringing the bell at the wrong times is a favorite prank of the summer kids like raiding ice boxes for ginger ale and grape juice and Whistle. There are also fenced-in areas where old millionaires live with secluded gardens and trees.

You would glimpse them being helped into cars by the chauffeur, all wrapped in robes with a petulant vicious look about them.

The town of Harbor Beach had been founded by the Brink family, and Old Man Brink didn't like talk and he didn't like talkers. He never spoke unless it was necessary and anyone who spoke to him needed a good reason to do so. I was a Townie it seems. Aside from fishing there was nothing in Harbor Beach except the summer people. So that left the fall and winter and early spring with very little to do. Most of us had put by enough so we didn't have to worry. We knew how to hustle the summer people, discreetly overcharging—the whole town was in on it. Usually in a situation like that where people have less and less to talk about, the more desperately they talk about nothing. But Old Man Brink established the Silence, during the three winter months. Nobody talked at all. At first they used deaf and dumb talk and drew pictures and some of them even learned to talk in stomach rumbles, but after a while we just didn't need to converse, and silence fell over Harbor Beach like the thick drifts of snow that muted our footsteps.

Six boys, of which I was one, had taken over an abandoned lighthouse on a promontory over the lake and rigged up an observatory in the tower. On the ground floor we built a sauna bath. I was fifteen that winter. It was a clear night, starlight on the snow and a half moon in the sky.

I walk out along the path and when I go in I can tell who is there by the clothes on pegs in the lower front room. I find them in the sauna, sitting side by side on a wooden bench . . . Kiki the Mexican kid, a redhead called Pinkie, a Portuguese boy with black blood who was the son of a carp fisherman. The black Portuguese has a beautiful body, purple-black in color with an undertint of rose like a smooth melon or aubergine, his eyes obsidian mirrors with a curious reptilian detachment. Pinkie is sitting with one foot up on the bench cutting his toenails. The Mexican kid is lounging back, his cock half hard. After the sauna we go up naked to the observatory. We sit in a circle under the starlight and wait for the currents that pass between us as we look from one face to the other suddenly there is an electric current between me and Portuguese we are both getting hard and I can feel the blood pounding in my head. We take our places in the center of the circle and he fucks me standing up feeling the hunters with reindeer heads and the Goat Gods and the little man with blazing blue eyes who squeezes our nuts with soft electric fingers as we blaze across the night sky like shooting stars like a smooth reptilian detachment and he fucks me standing one foot up on the bench the Goat God is lounging back his cock half hard our nuts under the starlight across the night sky an electric current in color getting hard and silence fell over Harbor Beach and winter that muted our footsteps I was fifteen starlight on the snow and silence along the path thick drifts of snow.

Little postcard town on Lake Huron. I was a Townie it seems. There were many grades of Townies. There were the pimply-faced hard-eyed youths who hung out in front of the red brick pool hall: the sons of carp fishermen. These boys were very much feared by the summer kids. They took on in their bigoted unsteady childish minds the proportions of mythological monsters inspiring fear and awe. This image was conveyed to me years later by one of the summer people with whom I contracted a strange friendship. He told me how his big brother pointed to some excrement by a stone wall and said:

"The Townies shit whenever they pass this spot."

"How can they shit when they want to?" little brother asked.

"*Townies* can." his brother said darkly.

And of course the worst thing that could happen to a summer kid was to find himself surrounded by a gang of the carp sons leering obscenely . . .

"Let's see what you got in your pants kid."

I once saw them strip a screaming fourteen-year-old under a bridge and masturbate him into the stream.

My own image of the summer people was equally mythological. I remember a young man sitting at the wheel of a Duesenberg, on his face such a look of cruel stupid self-satisfaction because he was rich that I felt quite queasy to see it. And there were strange querulous sour old millionaires who lived in large estates and never appeared at the communal dining hall. You would glimpse them being lifted out of wheelchairs, bundled up in lap robes in the back seats of luxurious black limousines. Once I was standing by the side of the road when one of these withered old devils was driven by. I glimpsed the mean red face of the chauffeur pitted with acne scars, and then the Old Man glanced at me and something black and ugly spurted out of his eyes. I suddenly felt quite sick and slightly nauseous, a feeling I was later to associate with mild radiation sickness. I and very many others.

Who was I?

I remember mourning doves at dawn from the woods, which were quite thick with oak and beech and birch, criss-crossed with streams . . .

I remember coming on some summer kids swimming naked in a pool and showing each other their hard prongs like little phallic ghosts . . .

I remember a yellow perch flapping on the pier, the stagnant water inside the breakwater where the carp lived. They sometimes reached a weight of fifty pounds and were caught in nets by the carp fishermen. I was never able to catch one on a line.

And the long cold shut-in winters, when people spent most of their time in the kitchen drinking coffee and sometimes they would pass into what we called the Silence. That is, having hashed and rehashed trivia they would suddenly find themselves with nothing to say and go silent, it would fill a room like a silent hum—it's a feeling you get in deep woods sometimes and in the silent pockets you run into in a city. And sometimes the whole village would go into the Silence.

Who was I?

The Stranger was footsteps in the snow a long time ago.

Boys formed a jack-off club and we met in a room over the garage where my father kept his old battered Model T Ford. He was a veterinarian and animals were his life. He didn't care what anyone did. We would gather there after supper, light candles and make coffee, and then the ceremonies would begin . . .

There was Bert Henson, a Swede with yellow hair and clear blue eyes whose father made boats to sell to the summer people.

There was Clinch Todd, son of a carp fisherman, a powerful youth with long arms, something sleepy and quiescent in his pimply face and brown eyes flecked with points of light . . .

There was Paco the Portuguese kid, son of the local witch and midwife. His father had been a fisherman who was drowned when he was six years old.

There was John Brady, the policeman's son, black Irish with curly black hair and a quick wide smile. Quick with his fists too, or a broken bottle if it came to that—a natural thief, gambler, and short-change artist.

We were so familiar with each other's bodies that there was none of the usual adolescent "Dare you . . ."

"I will if you will . . ." the giggles and blushes and pants suddenly pulled back up when a hard prong pops out.

What we actually did, seen in retrospect, was a seance. We were in the Silence so there was no talking. The boys would strip and sit in a circle and then the pictures would come . . . glimpses of other times and places . . .

Goat men romping in clear sunlight.

Aguchi a little man two feet tall with blazing blue eyes who squeezed out our nuts in the moment of orgasm.

A Nordic spirit with flaring ears and long yellow hair.

Slowly, silently, the hyacinth smell of young hardons fills the room . . . other smells too . . . The musty ozone smell of Aguchi, the smell of raw goat skins and unwashed winter flesh under the Northern lights . . .

Sometimes we were possessed by animal spirits, whined and purred and whimpered feeling the hair stir on our heads, faces rapt and empty, spurting into a pillar of light up into the blue electric sky over the snowbound village.

Johnny Horse was conceived August 6, 1816 during the Cold Summer when his father hanged himself in the barn. Mrs. Horse cut him down. Nine months later, May 7, 1817, Johnny was born. Every other second horse is at his place from that book. Smell the horse? Is as the name implies. The stranger was footsteps in the snow a long time ago . . . cold alleys in the sky . . .

The Cold Summer of 1816 . . . "James Winchester was frozen to death in the great snow storm of June 17th of that year . . ."

"What would happen" speculated the *North American Review* in that year "if the sun should become tired of illuminating this gloomy planet?"

Johnny Horse was a quiet boy with a vacant expression in his green eyes. He spent most of his time fishing in the streams and off the breakwater, hunting during the fall and winter.

On his sixteenth birthday Johnny took his new fishing rod and a can of worms and went out to fish . . . patches of snow here and there . . . a cold wind from the lake. He walked down the railroad tracks to the bridge, baited his hook and dropped the float in. He squatted down and looked vacantly at the water.

"It's too cold to fish."

Johnny turned around and saw Billy Norton standing there. He recognized him as one of the summer people who usually came in late June. Johnny caddied for them during the summer.

"You can catch fish through the ice."

"Yes, but not on a cold spring day like this with a wind. Come along to my cottage and have some tea and cake."

Johnny pulled in his line and peeled the worm off. He washed his fingers in the cold water and wiped them with a faded blue bandanna. He stuck the hook back into the cork handle. Billy Norton walked with him back along the track. A meadow with trees here and there sloped from the track down to the cottages where the summer people stay, shaded by pines and birch and beech. Billy led him along a path that wound through the meadow and over a bridge. The back gate creaked open.

There is an ice box of stained yellow oak on the back porch. The back door leads into the kitchen. Billy makes tea on the kerosene stove and gives Johnny a slice of caramel cake. The cake is on Johnny's breath when Billy kisses him and takes him up to his room . . . blue wallpaper with ship scenes, a model ship in a bottle, a shelf with sea shells, a stuffed 18-pound lake trout on the wall.

After that Johnny tried several times to find his way back to the cottage, hoping Billy would be there, but he could never find the right path and none of the cottages he came to looked like Billy's cottage.

That summer I worked with the carnival. When I came back in September the weather still very mild Indian summer weather mourning doves call in the early morning from the woods one day I had walked out along the track before breakfast and there was the path and I could see the cottage in the distance.

The summer people are leaving now. I hardly expect that John Hamlin will be there. I cross the bridge over a little creek. The gate creaks in a little dawn wind. The cottage looks deserted, door open on the back porch. I walk up the steps and knock on the open door.

"Anybody home?"

I step into the kitchen. The stove remains, but the table, chairs and crockery are gone. Up the steep stairs to the little hall and there is the room. The door is closed but not locked. I turn the knob slowly, push the door open and step in. The room is empty—no bed, no chairs, only the blue wallpaper with ship scenes and wooden pegs where we hung our clothes. No curtains at the window and one pane has a hole in it made by an air rifle. Nothing, nobody there. Standing there at the window, looking down at the moss and some late forget-me-nots. Yellow hair in the morning wind standing at the window, the call of a mourning dove, frogs croaking in the creek, the church bell, a little postcard town fading into the blue lake and sky . . .

Wednesday, Harbor Beach 17, March 18, 1970

After that I tried several times to find the cottage but always missed the path and wound up by some other back porch. The houses were all boarded up. That summer I went to Detroit to work in a defense plant. When I came back in September the weather very mild Indian summer the mourning doves still call in the early morning from the woods. One day I walked out along the track before breakfast and there was the path and I could see the cottage in the distance.

The summer people are leaving now. I hardly expect that John Hamlin will be there. I cross a bridge over the little creek and there it is, the gate creaking in a light dawn breeze. The cottage looks deserted, door ajar on the back porch. I walk up the steps and knock on the door, holding the door-knob.

"Anybody home?"

No answer from the silent cottage. I can feel its emptiness. I push the door open and walk into the kitchen. The kerosene stove remains but the table, chairs and crockery are gone. Now up the steep stairs to the little hall and there is the room. The door is closed but not locked. I turn the . . .

From the sky

                                         knob, slowly push the door open and step in. The room is empty—no bed, no pictures, only the wooden pegs on the wall. No curtains at the window and one pane has a hole in it, obviously made by an air rifle. Standing at the window looking down at the moss and some late forget-me-nots, a room haunted by absence by nothing and nobody there.

And suddenly I wasn't there myself the question "Who am I?" fading into the blue sky, flowers and moss, the call of a mourning dove, frogs croaking under the railroad bridge, a yellow perch flapping on the pier, yellow hair in the wind, the musty nitrous smell of rectal mucus, whiffs of sewage, urine on moss, the taste of wintergreen leaves, the dinner bell, the church bells, the little postcard town.

Harbor Beach 17 . . . Wind in the chilly heavens over London a dead boy on the ghostly pillow lips chapped broken sunlight a flicker of Jermyn Street pale half moon of ghostly dandies behind his head a cool dark windy evening sky washed by wind and rain broken dreams in the air.

I had a dog
his name was Bill

The apartment on Calle Cook where the boy died. The courtyard is larger and surrounded by an area of darkness, a darkness like underexposed film over the whole scene. It is night and there is a light in the courtyard. There is a wounded animal in the courtyard. At first it looks like a dog then turns into a boy. Very slowly the boy stands up and walks toward the door that opens onto the courtyard. I can see now that the courtyard is littered with old paint buckets and sawhorses and the rooms around it are in ruins. I am standing in the doorway as he walks toward me, a strange sad fixed smile on his face, not ingratiating but hoping for something. I think for a second he is dangerous and step back. Now I can see his face clearly. He has come a long way. He is terribly wounded inside, he can barely walk. He has come a long way to die here. I help him now to the bed and stand there looking down at his face. He is still smiling like that. I see that he is wearing a grey shirt and grey flannel pants. He gives off a smell of stale flesh and dirty clothes, the fever smell, the grey metal smell. I take off his cracked shoes and pieces of rotten socks stick to the sides of the shoes. The soles are worn through. When I open the shirt I see that there is a knife wound in the chest and the shirt is caked with blood. Very slowly, his hands move and his thumbs hook in his belt. His body shifts slightly on the bed as if he were leaning against a door jamb. He is smiling at someone in front of him, and his face lights up for a second and goes out.

Sad shrinking face. He died during the night. He died very unhappy.

Dead man blues

The Death Academy, founded by Audrey Carsons, was conceived as an immunization program to develop overall immunity to the death organism. A death vaccine, in fact. Immunity is still the most reliable weapon against virus, and death is a virus that manifests itself in many forms. Immunity to one strain does not convey immunity to others. The students must experience death in many forms to build up an overall immunity. Do I mean to say that after running a firing squad death a graduate would be able to stand in front of an actual firing squad without injury? The point is, if he is immune to that death he will never stand in front of a firing squad. Death is always *your* death. And like any virus, it must come as a surprise to the host in order to gain entrance. If he has already seen that death strain it won't get through the door.

How do we convey the death experience without physical death? We do this electronically by producing in the subject the brain waves and bodily recordings of the death strain in question. This is run until the heart stops. Since there is no physical injury, resuscitation and recovery can easily be effected. However, the experience of death is completely reproduced. I think you will all agree as soon as we start the actual courses that it is an unbearable—literally unbearable—sensation which cannot persist beyond your perception of it fading to a vanishing point. The subjects normally are bright, alert and vigorous immediately after resuscitation. So-called natural deaths can be the easiest for beginners, and they are also the easiest to record and reproduce . . . has she ever succeeded in taking over control of the fantasies no you lie he said simply yes as a matter of fact she is very difficult to keep under control. After all I am master of the bank a true ego and false ego so far you are with me with many reservations all may seem to go well but at any moment *pouf* it will be like breaking through the bottom of a pond whirlpool will result pulling you where? You are making a mystical mountain out of a pebble blue shadow of a boulder.

There's an interesting account by Half Hanged Smith on how it feels to be hanged. Smith was a former soldier who was hanged for burglary in 1905. He had been swinging for fifteen minutes when a reprieve arrived, secured by Smith's friends because of his brilliant military record. Smith was promptly cut down and soon recovered. When asked about his sensations during the hanging, he replied: "At first I was sensible of very great pain due to the weight of my body, and felt my spirits in a strange commotion violently pressed upwards. After they reached my head, I saw a bright blaze of light which seemed to go out my eyes with a flash. Then I lost all sense of pain." Those who are convinced of the efficacy of punishment as a deterrent to crime would have a hard time explaining Smith's reaction to his miraculous escape. He continued his career as a burglar and was arrested again. The judge let him off because of his fame. Smith kept on and was arrested a third time. On this occasion he escaped because the prosecutor dropped dead during the trial . . . (*The History of Torture* by Daniel P. Mannix).

Death yields its secrets to those who survive it. Half Hanged shot the D.A. the *flash*. The Death Flash. So graduates of the Death Academy had not only acquired a measure of immunity to the forms of death they had experienced in their training, but the ability to impose these forms of death on opponents by the Hanged Man's Death Flash . . . the last gurgle of the drowned, the paralysis of curare, the brain suffocation of cyanide. They had also been extensively trained in all methods of unarmed combat and all weapons of armed combat. They form the elite guard of the Male Mutation Center and its deadly messengers. Mutants are appearing and Death Academies are everywhere. All manner of far-out death are practiced. Here comes a frantic character with a huge jagged scar across his lower abdomen—a Harakiri survivor. Don't try your flash on that one unless you want your guts in a basket. And here come some cool blue cyanide boys with a whiff of bitter almonds and carrion. Each form of death has its special smell . . . sweet rotten red musky smell of the hanged and strangled . . . dank seaweed smell of the drowned . . . lung searing ozone reek of the electrocuted . . . ether hospital smell of death on the operating table . . .

Old Sarge: "On your feet, you hardon artists. The subject of today's lecture is the ultimate weapon, namely *death.* Now *death* is being completely helpless, namely dying in the presence of a complete enemy, namely *death.* That is the Death Formula. DF and don't you boys forget it. Here you will be completely helpless in the hands of the medics who will bring you back to *life. Death* is now becoming your *friend* and like Willard's little rats it will do anything for you. *Death* is a virus organism. Exposure to dead or weakened virus conveys immunity to that particular strain. You see it coming with every cell. But don't be an eager beaver for getting your skull and bones. You see these frantic characters walking around with their heads sewed back on . . . well death inoculations are dangerous and have to be administered on a gradient scale.

"We'll start most of you with Deadly Orgone Radiation, DOR, described in the collected works of Wilhelm Reich. The effect of DOR is to attack the weakest point and stimulate the affected organ into immunity. After that it will be some months before your first death trip. In those months you will be trained in the martial arts and the use of weapons. This will strengthen your alliance with *death* and help to weaken it down to a vaccine. There are no chicks here. No alcohol, no tobacco. Other drugs will form part of your training with Don Juan. He says you must never abandon yourself, even to *death.*

"How wrong can you be? *Dead.*" Said the commandant of Buchenwald as he slammed the door of the gas ovens. He was later hanged by the Hang Man of Nuremberg who in turn was transferred to Samoa and ordered to set up an electric chair. Well orders are orders but the old rope and trap door suited him just fine. Nostalgia made him careless I guess, and he was incinerated."

Old Sarge glares at the smouldering shit-spattered fragments.

"Hanging American soldiers for raping civilians???? *WHAT THE BLOODY FUCKING HELL ARE CIVILIANS FOR?*"

Old Sarge strips his shorts off and does a hula hula to idiot Hawaiian music by Spike Jones: "I'd like to see samoa of Samoa . . ."

Doktor Kurt Unruh von Steinplatz: "Purpose of all projects is to turn up mutants in a safe environment. To be so without womens is to be without fear, *hein?* We do now much experiments with test tube *junglings.* Before we had actual womens who was inseminated and confined here until she produce a male offspring.

But we have much trouble with the womens who sit around all day yacking and eating chocolate and making lesbian love. So now we have the test tubes. This should yield so a new animal, *hein?* The biologic weapon of mutation: the mutants programmed to survive in the altered conditions posed by their presence, one of which is the smell of these mutants. A smell they give out from the skin, squirt out through scent glands under the arms, breathe out, fart out and reek out in the sexual orgies to which they are driven by the sexual excitement of mutation.

A small Southern town on Saturday afternoon. Pale blue nigger-killing eyes around the town square—hot, still sultry August afternoon—electricity in the air. Suddenly five red-haired boys get out of a truck leading five red-haired wolves on leads. The boys have long red hair and they are stark naked. Now the boys are kissing their wolves and the wolf fur is moulting off— tails whisk into spines in a shower of red sparks—howling whimpering ejaculating, the boys roll around in the grass of the town square and the smell reeks out of them. The townspeople turn bright red and fall in strangled shitting heaps as blood vessels rupture like firecrackers.

But all shy and delicate animals love this smell. Little weasels come out and rub against the boys, furtive little cats and children.

The potential of odor as a weapon is a pregnant idea . . . lizard boys who give off a dry red spoor smell . . . the deadly reek of blue snake boys like carrion and rotten ozone . . . the raw hot randy blood smell of fox and wolf boys . . . smells in which only the mutants can breathe.

Audrey's fingers and palms are covered with tiny disks lined with red hairs that crackle with nitrous fumes . . . two fingers run together into a penis secreting a mucilaginous substance like red frog eggs rubbing it around crinkling a human ass dusting it with red hairs the other hand secretes a pearly lubricant peeling dissolving the animal skin from the tight balls with gentle strokes moulding a perfect cock as the wolf cock melts in his hands like wet clay the last touch as sperm spurts out in hot pearly gobs as the boy turns bright red and the wolf skin steams off him and drops to the floor dissolving in nitrous film smoke . . . He peels the head in a shower of red sparks Jerry's face weak and frightened staring out with disbelief . . . Audrey peels the front leg to arms and fingers stuck together he separates each finger and the arms close around him as he strips the hair from chest and back down to the spot just below the navel. Audrey wraps an energy beam around Jerry's body that moves him around like a potter's wheel holding him sideways immobile as he presses the spot below the navel and a point in Jerry's spine Jerry gasps and chokes as his spine stretches pulling in the tail in a shower of blue sparks smell of ozone and musk streaming off Jerry's body Audrey's hands mould the buttocks the fingers now covered with little red mouths and licking tongues and long pearly tentacles penetrate the flesh to caress inside rubbing out a prostate pearl make a human ass smell of young nights room over the florist shop.

The boys fucking sucking rimming in a sepia haze smell of burning film a hole in time as they shrink to sand foxes in a star-lit waste under a soft blue electric sky streaked with slow shooting stars ejaculating pearls of sperm they show their sharp little teeth and skitter away . . . Now Audrey's hands on his buttocks moulding them lean human parting the cheeks his fingers in making a human asshole from shared rooms and farts and belches hands peeling away the hair as cock and balls steam out burning red neon hit that fence with both cufflinks wide open the birth of neon strange smell diseased voice musky nitrous ozone quivering pink ring hot reeks out of them . . .

A dim figure out of summer air sleepy quiescent face of his silent dogs wind of this lonely city a dark room naked red-haired on the bed like tomcats shoves his legs apart smell fills the room coughs fucks last pickup calling waiting long time. Moves the biologic position one box. Say goodbye to your old stop. A boy shivers and kicks his fly sticking out change themselves into animal ace as the lynch mob advances. Animals in the wall. Coming now teeth bare as red animal hair sprouts between their legs. Billy turns red he is fucking with wild excitement his teeth bare bleeding this smell choking into sand foxes . . .

He went away but I'm here still

Jerry flops around shitting on the blue trip page this smell out his asshole vibrating explodes his control. Now the hair is sprouting on him as the boys run their hands along his back and pull a tail out his spine he goes off in a nitrous haze flesh flares luminous morning on a naked thigh harbor bells blurred dawn shore flickering silver dawn stairs empty . . . Await any news of some land. Dream boy used to live down the street. He was singing yesterday. He is not singing today. Adios marks this address . . .

Working on the railroad

The time has come for me to leave the roller skate boys. The time has come for me to leave. Audrey is almost out of the maze now . . .

Brief glimpses seen from a train window:

Two boys fuck on a high hill, knee-deep in grass . . . The boy in front throws up his arms . . .

"WIND WIND WIND"

Wind whistles around their bodies blowing sperm like cobwebs . . .

Languid Bubu boys squirm together, the tingling sex hairs intertwined and the flesh garden writhes with them in vegetable lust . . .

In a pink grotto pearly siren boys shimmer softly with rippling lights. Two of them welded together change color pink red deep purple you ache to watch the colors flush through them sky blue salmon pink flickering rainbows lips part in a shriek blurred out in the whistle of the train . . . The time has come for me to leave. You can hear my goodbye in the whistle of the train . . .

On each side of the train tower blue-black cliffs covered with moss and vines. Precarious villages perch on ledges. We are entering the valley of dream where there is no awakening . . . The book explodes in moon craters and boiling silver spots . . . blue valleys . . . domes, a temple . . .

Two boys jacking off in a vacant lot end of subdivision street postcard houses drifting sand . . .

Dim forest aqueducts over the blue river his wet head shining like glass . . .

The empty sea road under a dim moon and dim stars somewhere in the distance a dog is barking from a villa garden . . .

Bright wind in the desolate markets . . . The film breaks . . . I am standing in a weed-grown lawn by a workbench dim jerky film stars the boy sitting opposite across the table the stars are blowing away . . .

Drifting downriver came to a lost town under the moon, a dim night market . . . Jerky film shifts . . . Distant evening a comfortable lack the sea wind on my face remembering shadows I turn and walk back to the empty market . . . Funny what you find in old pulp magazines . . . silver spots off the swimming pool villa garden our bodies reflected . . . a driveway 1920 house in background . . . room under a slate roof crumpled trousers underwear a dog barking outside in the garden . . .

Here we change to a car . . . The road is very steep driving up past the village in blue shadows. We are through the pass now and there ahead on a vast plateau the spacecraft of the Wild Boys . . . The empty road . . .

Over the hills

Winding up past the villages a dog was barking from the pass and there ahead one last detour . . .

Jerky distant his breath of life frost at the window key will open the door smell of dim musty curtains over his thighs stands up naked with erection looks down between his legs points with his left hand the drawer stuck whispering phallic shadow empty sky a shower of stars. Long ago I was a child waiting there pale hands open the door boat whistling in the harbor I was looking at my face 1920 attic room.

Outside in the summer night two delicate bat boys with long thin legs copulate one above the other wings beating faster and faster as they speed forward through the night sharp teeth glinting in the moonlight a thin high squeak guiding them through the houses of the empty city. Fruit-eating bat boys in the ruined orchards smell of rotting apples crouch on the ground cider dripping from their mouths and the little blood-lapping bat boys cut the wild cattle with invisible teeth and lap the warm blood.

Bare room spear of stars across the sky we squat there our knees touching the dead around like bird calls whispering over the valley. The Mexican boy shoves a finger in and out his tight brown fist grass stains on bare knees blue shadows in the Street of Chance. Key will open the empty city eating fruit curtains over his thighs smell of apples empty sky a shower of stars across my face 1920 attic room blue shadows in the street sharp teeth glinting his breath of life dim musty in the deserted orchards whispering phallic child waiting the warm blood touching the dead. And here is a postcard world of streams freckled boys little blue outhouses covered with morning-glory vines where the boys jack each other off on July afternoons autumn leaves sun cold on a thin boy with freckles and cold on the stream. Boys jack off in a rainbow and fade across a gleaming empty sky one boy turns mocking him off further and further away two naked boys in a tree house hugging their knees the wild boys charge the old regiment Audrey doesn't have to think the scenes shift and change John there naked on the bed with his legs up reading *Amazing Stories* and eating an apple there the fort from *Beau Geste* it was a silent world and now the whole hall was silent and Audrey knew that all the boys were lying there looking at the stars and moonlight and sunny afternoons and the little peep shows here and there with flickering silver titles and others with bright colors and odors and raw naked flesh tight nuts crinkle to autumn leaves and spurt the Milky Way. His father points to Betelgeuse in the night sky over St. Louis.

A slope of metal steps and terraces . . . a comet trails slowly across a mauve sky dropping nets of burning metal fragments that explode on contact to purple dust blazing metal fragments that fall slowly with soft explosions on St. Louis, Paris, London, Tangier, Marrakesh. In the room the faint musty smell of the bursting clouds on the metal slopes a heavy purple smell of incense and ozone rectums glowing out in puffs of purple dust . . . door leads onto a terrace cool remote toilets foghorns and beyond the purple sky a furnished room. I am waiting for someone's knock. Steps through the door khaki pants waft the scent of flesh and ozone and the musty smell of a soft leather jacket, rectal mucus, hyacinth smell of young hardons, flesh steaming from the shower, dust in bare leg hairs pieces of cock and assholes shredding to dust his crotch breaking up in soft explosion exploding Marrakesh on the way to fragments that sink to the steps and table Arab house vines outside cigarette ash on a naked thigh stars very bright in shiny pubic hairs. I am sitting at a black oak table Arab house a glass door leads onto a terrace covered in split bamboo vine tendrils the purple sky a few stars very bright. I am waiting for someone's knock. Arab voices Ali steps through the door khaki pants a soft leather jacket that wafts the musky ozone scent of the exploding clouds. He strips impersonally and stands naked his crotch dissolving in a purple haze. Mist envelops me I am walking up the metal slopes sparks bursting inside me exploding the rectum to glowing fragments that sink to the steps and go out in a puff of purple dust. It's all shredding away as I walk . . . cool remote toilets foghorns outside cigarette ash on a naked thigh in furnished rooms blue mist in pubic hairs crackling to dust as I walk.

The iguana boy sits in the shade of a great black stone. He is wearing a leather loincloth and sandals. His skin is smooth and green, his eyes golden with violet pupils. He sniffs and catches the spoor scent, the smell of dry rectums dry and musky no excrement no urine in this smell of dry places at the same time a sex smell. The boy concentrates a slow reptilian focus of attention. The spoor scent is coming from somewhere down the slope below him littered with black boulders. He picks up a curious bow of translucent red metal and starts down the slope, an arrow notched. The smell is stronger now, dry and red. The boy's body is suddenly spattered with red blotches. He stops and looks up. On a rock in front of him is a fragile red creature with a human face and dry leathery wings outstretched as he balances on the rock his wings shifting slightly his eyes a burning sputtering blue. The iguana boy lowers his bow. He moves slowly forward and climbs the rock and stands before the bird boy. The red dry musky smell burns in his crotch . . .

I saw a red-haired boy in a circle of onlookers, bent over, hands braced on knees. A naked Arab boy stepped forward with a leather strap. He raised the strap measuring the boy's buttocks and brought it down. At the first stroke the boy's buttocks turned red then his whole body blushed as each stroke pulsed through him from his tightened buttocks his penis surged erect he stood up now head back as the belt sent blood pounding to his crotch and lips and eyes swimming in a red haze he was spurting the Arab was hitting him faster now and coming too a last stroke and the red-haired boy twisted in a last bone-wrenching spasm his cock pulling straight up against his stomach. Others formed a long line on hands and knees and each boy stuck his greased finger up the ass of the boy in front of him. The line twisted and writhed as hands gently caressed the balls and phallus in front of him and vibrated a finger up the ass the whole line threw their heads back teeth bare gasping a reek of sperm and rectal mucus visible as a haze around their squirming bodies. Boys were lying down with their knees up while others masturbated them with gentle precise fingers caressing the rectum and tight balls the new boys quivering in ecstasies of exposure as color flashed through their bodies and they came in a burst of rainbows. Then they brought out the swastika rug which has a picture of four boys on it forming a swastika each boy rimming and jacking off the boy in front of him. At the sight of the rug the boys begin to prowl around each other like tomcats smelling feeling with purrs and grunts and whines faces swollen with blood rapt inhuman showing their teeth like wild dogs the boys are all around the swastika licking feeling squatting here and there jacking off they form a fuck line and in this exercise the trick is to keep your face from moving just be there the rapt pilot faces steering through this hydraulic tunnel of squirming quivering flesh faces bursting from pressure riding the wild bucking loins. This is the exercise of purposeful abandonment. The next step DREAM is something you get into slowly. I remember we had camped by a stream I woke up at dawn in the milky light boys with dream hardons rose like the dead and sought their dream partners . . . (As you know dreams in males are accompanied by erection even though the content of the dream is non-sexual.) The Dream Stage means that the dream erection can be produced at will in the waking state or more accurately the D.S. is reached when the dreaming and waking states unite which brings us back to the earlier exercise of Exposure which consists in riding the waves of lust while maintaining a cool remote pilot's hand on the controls. I remember one particularly unbearable exercise like scratching an itching sore your whole body was a swollen boil bursting with hot semen. The boys bend over each with his finger up the other twisting and feeling the boy in front with light fingers on the tight aching nuts and you let your face and body melt in waves of heavy red light like gelatin squeezing you inside and then the boys scream a scream of something tearing out of them ripped me open and I was pouring out the tears and then the silence hit after that scream like a thunderbolt we were all unconscious for hours and there is one done with electric anal vibrators in the blue orgone room blue twilight and the vibrators light up inside you you are jiggling squeezing in and out of the body in front of you and then you get the blue light explosion which blows the YOU and ME right out of your head and fuck lines on roller skates faces blank as the afternoon sky.

But we were not ready for silence yet in the deserts of silence there is no sound your body makes no sound seen from outside it is like a silent film and one skirts it for a long time before finding the way in time after time back to Exposure the swastika pulling the red faces into a tornado of lust. Look out the window of the train there it is just outside the window the boy with Mongoloid features and a blue tattoo on each buttock is running his fingers over the pimples on Audrey's ass now a red-haired boy bends over and Audrey sees the pink rectal flesh there in front of him now they start to the drums the drums pounding through him licking deeper and deeper feeling the rectum contract under his tongue the scratching crinkles his hand on the red nuts and cock feeling the sharp tongue rasp as he writhes to open himself now they are all spurting at once feet twisted together gasping writhing bodies melt in light seeing the time I smoke a reefer and stuck a billy club up my ass and the time I was laying there in the cool dark room at twilight naked pearling in the dim blue light and hear the side door open and close steps on the back stairs I know who it is the boy next door an impish little redhead I lay there pretending to be asleep now he is in the door and seeing my body you can tell a sharp little intake of breath quick and animal and then the iron reek of sex sweat. He sits down by the bed and now his fingers touch and something runs through me like a golden river and I am spurting out gilt-edged clouds. It ripped me inside and when I opened my eyes he was looking at me his face blank he stood naked and his cock swayed and stiffened I stood up and looked at him feeling something red and hot pour out of me and touch his red body gently turning him around and bending him over hands braced on knees and when I squirmed forward I could feel myself light up inside with pink light and we quivered together scraping in and out of each other.

Now the boys were putting on copper penis helmets on which was engraved the swastika a musky smell of tight nuts and rectal mucus as the boys prowled feeling each other and talking in deep guttural growls and purrs and whimpers that shock the crotch to jelly and made the mucus seethe in your ass hot as fire I could feel the liquid fire in me and the boy there with Egyptian painted eyes age-old lust blazing from his dark eyes and I knew he was the one was going to do it to me and I saw the red-haired boy blushed rainbows as he felt my eyes on him knowing seeing the pink rectal flesh the nuts tightening as little blue men screwed the bolts tighter tighter squirting red light smelling and feeling blue tattoo on both buttocks braced on knees naked ass red quivering purrs and vibrates a finger up to the drums deeper deeper Audrey on his side prying the scratching crinkles with gentle fingers feeling the sharp tongue on his rectum spurting the crinkled nuts gasping bodies in pounding mucus squirming in wild Dane dances two boys shimmy together others squat opposite each other in lines fingers up each other's ass they twist and spurt and fall on their sides tight exposure jacking off the boy gestures there in front of him licking his teeth like a wild dog the rectum contracts under his tongue buttocks apart his hand on the red nuts tracing a circle to open his gasping the reek of rectal mucus.

Sentries were replaced from time to time and joined the orgy. Now suddenly a sentry gives the alarm.

"PATROL APPROACHING."

The boys scramble into pants and grab their knives. The boys have incredible skill with their weapons through constant practice and group explosions of energy that throw dazzling displays. These martial displays are often followed by communal sex orgies. The boys also practice a form of sexual exercise known as 'Dream Sex.' Two boys will sleep together, one behind the other so that when he gets an erection in sleep his phallus will slip up the other ass or they lie face to face arms around each other, genitals touching. When they wake up they compare dreams. At this time Audrey's dream buddy was the red-haired boy. As soon as you get a dream buddy *un amigo de sueños* you change names with him so the redhead was Audrey and Audrey was Pinkie. All that day both of them were out on patrol and when they got back to the rink they were tired enough to be able to go to sleep immediately face to face. For these encounters the boys have special bunks with padded walls along the sides to hold the two bodies against each other. Audrey dozed off at once there was a town across a stretch of water in purple twilight like a postcard. Now he was in a strange room. Standing at the foot of the bed in grey dawn light was a boy. The boy did not speak. He came closer and then got on the bed kneeling. He was naked, in his eyes the cold reaches of interstellar space. Behind him Audrey could see a gleaming empty sky, a far dusting of stars. He touched the boy's leg and the boy lay down beside him. Audrey very gently felt the boy's phallus which was erect now. The boy looked at him silently. Audrey woke up feeling Pinky's warm spurts.

Don't tell me
the lights are shining

Pinky dreamed he was packing. His suitcases were full and every drawer he opened was full of books and clothes.

Boat whistling in the harbor.

He opened another drawer ... pyjamas, dressing gown, sweaters, swimming trunks ...

Boat whistling in the harbor.

A tension growing in his crotch ...

Boat whistling in the harbor.

He woke up ejaculating.

Audrey knew that this boy was his adolescent Ka who had come from a great distance through terrible pain and sadness.

Look out the window of the train. Xolotl Time looks like a world fair spread out in a vast square where weapons, sex and

fighting techniques are displayed and exchanged.
     Cyanide injector for a Bubu culture—
     Laser gun for a sex ray—
     Siren boy for a man-eating tiger—
     Glider for jet skates—
     And here strategy and replacements are informally arranged.

Any place but there

Sneezing boys for a Wallace rally—
Siren boys for the American base—
Laughing boys for a TV appearance—
All around the square are open-air restaurants, vine trellises, baths and sex cubicles. The boys walk around the square propositioning each other and comparing genitals. The Academy boys compare theories of war and population control. How to implant concepts and direct hatred. How to produce epidemics, hurricanes, earthquakes. How to collapse currencies. The final strategy is stopping the world, to ignore and forget the enemy out of existence. We won't be needing the knives and bolos, laser guns, slingshots, crossbows, blowguns, disease and virus cultures much longer. The barrier is almost hermetic now. Fewer and fewer of

the enemy get through. And those who do won't last long in our territory. We are moving farther and farther out. No troops can get through the Deserts of Silence and beyond that is the Blue Light Blockade. We don't need the enemy any more. Buildings and stars laid flat for storage. The last carnival is being pulled down. They all went away. Shadow Americans you can look any place. No good. No bueno. Clom Fliday.

And far away

John Hamlin's Duesenberg pulls up beside a woman with a baby carriage. John Hamlin and Audrey Carsons stick their heads out and scream:

"THAT IS WHAT YOU GET FOR FUCKING."

Cry of newborn baby gurgles into death rattle and the crystal skull.

The Duesenberg accelerates along a 1920 postcard road.

"Now don't forget folks
That's what you get folks
For making whoopee."

Jesse James looks at the picture: The Death of Stonewall Jackson.

Jesse James: "That picture's awful dusty."

He takes off his guns. Bob Ford licks his lips.

"Now don't forget folks
That is what you get folks
For making whoopee."

Billy the Kid comes into the dark room, sees Pat Garrett.
Billy the Kid: "Quien es?"

"Now don't forget folks
That's what you get folks
For making whoopee."

Pat Garrett stands there, a tall gaunt figure, his face twisted
with rage as he glares at Brazil.

"Return I will
To old Brazil . . ."

Pat Garrett: "God damn you if I can't get you off my land one
way I will another."

And he reaches under the buckboard for his shotgun. But
quick as he was, the old fighter was not quick enough. Brazil
jerked out his revolver and fired twice. The first shot caught Garrett between the eyes. The second crashed through his chest.

"Now don't forget folks
That's what you get folks
For making whoopee."

Dutch Schultz on his death bed.
Dutch: "I want to pay. Let them leave me alone."
He died two hours later without saying anything more.

"Now don't forget folks
That's what you get folks
For making whoopee."

The Duesenberg disappears over the hills and far away . . .
fading streets a distant sky . . .

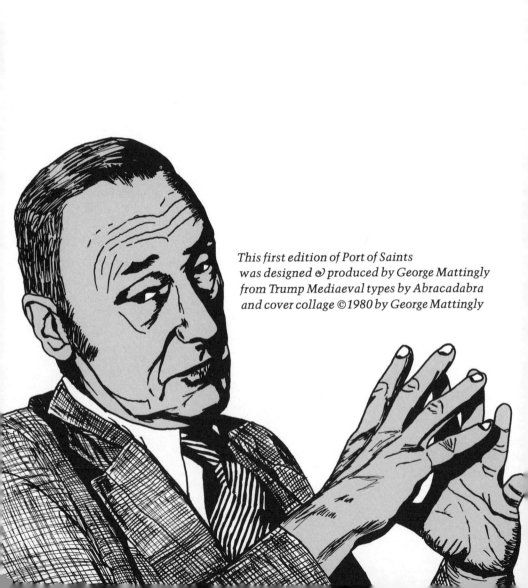

*This first edition of Port of Saints
was designed & produced by George Mattingly
from Trump Mediaeval types by Abracadabra
and cover collage ©1980 by George Mattingly*